Connections 8   THE GIFT OF TIME   Paul Stuart

www.connectionsbooks.co.uk

THE GIFT of TIME

by

PAUL STUART

Best wishes

Connections 8   THE GIFT OF TIME   Paul Stuart

This edition first published in November 2018

Paul Stuart asserts his right to be identified as the author of this work under the Copyright, Designs and Patents Act 1988.

This is entirely a work of fiction. The names, characters and incidents portrayed within it are the work of the author's imagination. Any resemblance to actual persons, living or dead, events or localities is purely coincidental.

ISBN: 978-0-244-43250-8

All rights reserved. This book is sold subject to the condition that it shall not be resold, lent, hired out or otherwise circulated without the express prior consent of the author and/or the publisher.

Connections 8   THE GIFT OF TIME   Paul Stuart

ALSO BY PAUL STUART

Paperbacks:
Connections 1 -Who Did You Sit Next To Today?
Connections 2 -Hell Has No Fury
Connections 3 -That's None of Your Business
Connections 4 -Which Room Did You Stay In?
Connections 5 –I Need a Word
Connections 6 –An Extraordinary Life
Connections 7 –Stones in my Jar

Hardbacks:
The Mobile and the Ring - The John Lomax Story
The Mobile and the Ring - The John Lomax Story (Limited Edition Hardcover)
Lomax and the Biker - The Complete Trilogy (Limited Edition Hardcover)
The Exmoor Trilogy – (Limited Edition Hardcover)
Stones in my Jar – (Limited Edition Hardcover)

Connections 8   THE GIFT OF TIME   Paul Stuart

AUTHOR'S NOTE

I've always enjoyed writing and have been lucky enough to have managed to produce some novels, but this is my first attempt at writing short fiction for publication.

All storytelling has, as its most important goal, emotionally engaging the audience as much as possible. I don't want to come away from reading a book or seeing a film and think, 'wasn't that interesting?' I want to think: 'I need to calm down, take a breath, allow the stitch in my side to ease from the laughter or let the tears subside.' In short, I want to be captivated by art and entertainment.

In novels, this level of intensity is accomplished by creating multi-dimensional characters and throwing each into his or her own roller-coaster subplots that are rife with reversal and escalating levels of conflicts, which are ultimately resolved. In short stories, an author doesn't have the time or space to follow this formula. But short fiction still needs to captivate, to enthrall. One way to do this is to go for the gut with a shocking twist, a surprise, the unexpected.

One thing I like about short stories is that they allow an author to step out of genre more easily than novels do. Finally, for the reader, there is less of a commitment when reading short fiction and this may suit our modern lifestyles.

Connections 8   THE GIFT OF TIME   Paul Stuart

FOREWORD

There are times in life when you feel like giving up. As I sit and compose this Foreword I look back at the last few months and wish I could do just that.

My wife suffered a fall on the Chapter House steps at the rear of Truro cathedral on 3rd June, 2018. She was in front of me when she tripped, turned over onto her back and fell, head first, down the metal edged steps. Her head struck every single step and I can see her now and hear the thumps. She didn't call out and she didn't cry. She just lay there, with her eyes open, gasping for breath as her arms reached out. I held her hands as blood seeped from her fractured skull and began to bubble from her mouth and nose.

Many people were quick to help and she was, after what seemed to me an eternity, taken by ambulance to hospital. As she lay on a spinal board, about to be lifted, a jobs-worth with a clipboard and pen loudly issued an instruction to "get this mess cleared up." He was fortunate that I was too much in shock, and not near enough to him, to react.

I stayed at her bedside for two days and nights, refusing to leave. I suppose I was hoping for a miracle, but I knew in my heart what was about to happen. She didn't regain consciousness, but I'm convinced she could hear me as I whispered and begged and pleaded and stroked her lovely soft, fine hair, held her delicate hands and kissed her sweet lips.

Connections 8   THE GIFT OF TIME   Paul Stuart

I was not alone, of course. Her youngest daughter kept vigil for as long as she could and her eldest grandchild insisted on being with her beloved Grandma for as long as she was able. Brave young fifteen-year old girl. Just a few days beforehand she had danced a jig of joy in our living room at finally having grown taller than her Grandma.

Many friends appeared, as if by magic, at Jan's bedside and laid tender hands on my shoulder, hugged me with meaningful warmth and whispered words of comfort in my ear. My mobile phone was alive, it seemed, and I eventually turned it off, not wanting anything to disturb my last, precious moments with my wonderful Jan.

The Critical Care Unit at RCHT Treliske is a special place. Its staff are professional, yet caring in a very personal way. No divas, just a wonderful team of incredible individuals, doing what needs to be done with soft and tender compassion. And the uplifting thought that Jan helped others, unknown and anonymous to us, with the gift of organ donation brought solace and still does.

As it all unfolded and since that awful time, my friends, my real friends, the stones in my jar, have stood by me and nursed me through.

Canon Simon Bone seemed to know the right times to appear, whether it was day or night. He gave, and continues to give, strength to me in my darkest hours. He speaks or sends a text every day, even whilst on holiday. I am honoured to count him as a friend.

Connections 8   THE GIFT OF TIME   Paul Stuart

Simon, Owen, Janet (Jan's lifelong friend) and Geoff, Carolyn, Debbie and Sam, Pam and Derek, Tim and Lorraine, Christine and Neal. Everybody from within our wonderful community at St.Piran's Church, Perranarworthal and beyond. Lovely friends from Sainsbury's, Slimming World, the knitting group, the Friends of RCHT Treliske at the Sunrise Centre and the ladies of the Look Good Feel Better unit. Peter and Linda from The White Horse at Exford, Nina and Martin and now Karen. I could go on ad infinitum.

At the heart of it all, holding me together as chaos threatened to take over, were my Mum, Dad and sister, Helen. They were and still are, I know, deeply shocked by what happened and yet were somehow able to summon the strength to give me incredible support, despite their own difficulties. I am blessed to have all these people with me as I try to understand what has happened and why. The one thing I do understand is that I need a larger jar.

Twenty-two years of the deepest love two people can show each other torn from us in a matter of seconds, and yet all these people have sown the seeds of how to carry on.

I still cry every day, often many times each day, and the grinding loneliness as I close the front door behind me or open letters addressed to Jan, is often too much to bear.

And yet, I can hear Jan whispering encouragement and urging me to continue writing; to complete this book; not to waste time.

Connections 8   THE GIFT OF TIME   Paul Stuart

The theme that runs through each of these stories is time. It rules all our lives. It is the one constant for us all. We dance to its tune with every breath we take from the moment we are born. The wise amongst us learn to use it to our advantage and I can hear and feel her urging me to do just that. I am sure she is with me, smiling her beautiful quiet smile.

And so, here it is. The most difficult book I've ever written. "The Gift of Time" from Jan.

Connections 8   THE GIFT OF TIME   Paul Stuart

THE IMPORTANCE OF TIME	10
GAME: A YEAR AGO	79
GAME: PRESENT DAY	93
USE TIME WISELY	110
SPLIT SECONDS COUNT	173
A WEEK IN TIME	205

Connections 8   THE GIFT OF TIME   Paul Stuart

THE IMPORTANCE OF TIME

PROLOGUE

In her pocket, Emily had a little plastic boat. Around her neck, she had the necklace that Books gave her at Christmas. On her wrist, she had the delicate shell bracelet that a little girl gave her. Emily's jar was filling nicely. Each item had a special meaning for her.

The boat and bracelet were gifts from two young children who had needed to know that their father was a man to be proud of. Emily couldn't bring him back, but she could, and did, give them reason for pride and love. She hoped it would stand them in good stead for the rest of their lives.

She fingered the necklace and felt the familiar warm glow of tenderness and love that it gave her. It was a present from Books, and just touching it and thinking of him always brought the same warm glow, which was also always accompanied by the same beautiful moist feeling in certain of her more personal areas. It never failed to make her smile. If others experienced the same emotions, she thought to herself, then they were lucky indeed.

Connections 8 THE GIFT OF TIME Paul Stuart

-1-

Standing patiently in the queue, hand in hand, Emily and Books inched forwards towards the entrance. She smiled as he tickled her palm with a finger and fought to supress a girly giggle. He held firm as she tried to wriggle her hand free and looked around, pretending nothing was happening.

"Will you behave yourself?" she whispered.

"No," he replied, with a grin as broad as the pavement they were standing on.

"I will do something, you know." Emily laughed, stressing the word 'will.'

"Like what?" He challenged.

"Ah, I didn't say here and now, did I? Revenge will be mine when you least expect it," she promised. "I will serve it cold."

"There are times when you frighten me, and times when you don't," Books mocked as he disengaged his hand and put his arm around her waist. Before she knew it, she felt a cold hand under her clothing. He playfully pinched her flesh and pulled her towards him to prevent retaliation.

"Ouch!" she cried, and leaned in to him, feeling his warmth and muscular strength. "There'll be trouble," she promised.

"You and whose army?" he replied.

"Just me. I don't need an army. Just you wait and see." She looked up at him and ran the tip of her tongue suggestively across her slightly parted lips.

"Home now?" he asked, hopefully.

"Oh no. I haven't stood in this queue for nearly half an hour just to walk away now. I want to see this film. It's the premiere and I'm not leaving now. Patience grasshopper."

Officially they were on leave. Not that it meant much, as they were always available when necessary. They had certainly earned a break after the "Stones in my Jar" drama. Emily's body was recovering well from her encounter with fire and ice. She was not in pain any more, but wasn't keen on going through such extremes again. Her burns and grafts were healing nicely and the evidence of her various other physical injuries had almost gone. The psychological damage was another matter, though. She needed all the help she could get as she continued her recovery. Above all, she needed her lovely man. He was hers and God help anybody who interfered with that.

They realised they had allowed a space to develop in front of them and people were looking. Sheepishly they closed the gap quickly in case anybody tried to fill it. There were only about twenty people in front of them now.

Books began to rummage around in his pocket, feeling for loose change, and, just at that moment, Emily's mobile phone buzzed. She jumped at the sound. She rarely received text messages that were marked with exclamation marks. It was uncharacteristic of her father to adorn messages with such paraphernalia, being much more prone to understatement, but when she read the text and

Connections 8   THE GIFT OF TIME   Paul Stuart

saw that it told her over a hundred people were going to die in two hours she understood the need. She held the mobile up towards Books and indicated with her eyes that he should look at it.

Books' face was immediately stern. He returned the phone to Emily. She made the call.

"Details?" she asked. No time or need for beating around the bush.

"Go on," she instructed.

"Sorry, Emily, this is bad. We're needed. It seems there's an outfit planning an attack of some description. They've promised an update in fifteen minutes. I need you and Books now."

They had been in the queue for three-quarters of an hour and were reluctant to leave, but the urgency in Frank's voice convinced them.

"We can be with you in twenty minutes," Emily said.

"Not good enough," her father replied. "You see that Jaguar across the road, sitting on the double yellow line? Jump in. The driver is waiting."

Emily and Books swung their heads in unison, as if in an Olympic synchronised swimming competition. They looked at each other and dashed across the road, bringing a taxi to a screeching halt amid a volley of cockney abuse. They heard a crunch as something failed to avoid contact with the taxi.

Just as they both hit the leather rear seats, Emily's phoned buzzed into life again.

"That wasn't fifteen minutes," Emily observed.

Connections 8   THE GIFT OF TIME   Paul Stuart

"I know," her father replied. "It seems they have an elastic sense of time."

"So what is it?" Emily was in work mode now.

"An attack of some kind. The voice was vague and wouldn't give anything more about what type of attack. Could be IED, chemical, shooting, a vehicle. Anything. But they were sure the victims would number a hundred at least. Oh, it also turns out they have a mole in the security services, which is why we're being used. They won't know of our existence. They'll think they're dealing with our security services." Frank paused to allow the import of his information sink in.

"Is it up and running?" Emily asked.

"Yes," her father replied. "Hence the time limit."

"Anything else?" Emily needed more details.

"He's called Quarim. He's their mouthpiece. He said they were heading back now, and the attack would be at four this afternoon." Frank said.

"And we've no idea about location?" Emily asked.

"No," said her father.

"You said they were heading back now," Emily grabbed at the only information she'd been given.

"Yes. We put a trace on the mobile, so we know where they were when the call was made. But he may not have been anywhere near where the attack will be. But, it's a start. Also, we think Quarim was in a BMW. Somebody swore at him from another car because he was driving and using his

Connections 8   THE GIFT OF TIME   Paul Stuart

mobile at the same time and then reported the number plate to the locals. He said there were two of them in the car. Thank God for the great British public, eh? We've got everybody available looking for it now."

Emily listened intently. She caught her reflection in shop windows as they sped by. It was like the early cinema with its images flickering so rapidly that they merged into a continuous film. She waved at herself and saw the strobe effect.

Books was on his own phone by now and listening hard. Their driver half turned to announce that a white BMW had been stopped and surrounded. He didn't know where. It could be London or anywhere in the UK.

"No shooting," Emily shouted at her mobile. "I don't want either of them killed. They need to meet Books."

Connections 8   THE GIFT OF TIME   Paul Stuart

-2-

The venue was good. The large windows of the banqueting room at the hotel looked out over the beach. Although, right now the beach had that December afternoon look to it: bleached, dusty, though the haze was mostly mist with a bit of fog thrown in. Not so focused, but, hey, a beach view beat a motorway view any day, provided the sun held.

"Harry," Tanya said to her associate. "You think we need more tables over there? It looks empty."

Tanya, President of the local business association, was a woman in her sixties and a grandmother several times over. Although her employer was one of the larger institutions that had misbehaved a bit a few years ago, she'd had no part in the matter of mortgage-backed securities. She believed firmly that banks were a force for good. She wouldn't have been in the business if she didn't think that. She was living proof of the beneficence of the world of finance. Tanya and her husband had comfortable retirement funds thanks to banks, her daughter and son-in-law had expanded their graphic arts business and made it successful thanks to banks, her grandsons would be going to the best private schools and top universities thereafter, without the encumbrance of student loans. The earth revolved around money, but that was a good thing. Far better than guns and battleships, and she was happy and proud to be a part of the process.

Connections 8   THE GIFT OF TIME   Paul Stuart

The diminutive, white-haired woman wouldn't have been in the business for forty-six years if she'd felt otherwise.

Harry Smith, who she considered as her second-in-command, was a heavyset man with a still face, a lawyer specializing in commercial paper and banking law. He eyed the corner she was pointing to and agreed.

"Asymmetrical," he said. "Can't have that."

Tanya tried not to smile. Harry took everything he did quite seriously and was a far better 'i-dotter' than she. Asymmetrical would be a sin, possibly mortal. She walked up to the two hotel employees who were organizing the room for the Christmas party, which would last from three to five today, and asked that they move several of the round tables to cover the bald spot on the banquet room floor. The men rearranged them and Harry nodded.

Tanya said, "Not asymmetrical now."

Her underling laughed. Taking his tasks seriously didn't mean he was devoid of a sense of humour. Harry took the room in.

"Looks good to me. Double-check the sound system. Then we'll get the decorations up."

"The PA?" she asked. "I tried it yesterday. It was fine." But being the 'i-dotting' banker that she was, Tanya walked to the stage and flicked on the PA system. Nothing. She tried a few more flicks of the on/off button, as if that would do any good.

"This could be a problem."

Connections 8   THE GIFT OF TIME   Paul Stuart

Tanya followed the wire but it disappeared below the stage.

"Maybe those workers," Harry said, peering at the microphones.

"Who?"

"Those two who were here a half-hour ago. Maybe before you got here?"

"No, I didn't see anybody. Josh and Mike?" she asked, nodding at the men on the hotel staff, now setting up chairs.

"No, other ones. They asked if this is where the banking meeting was going to be. I told them yes and they said they had to make some repairs under the stage. They were under there for a few minutes, then they left."

She asked the two hotel workers in the corner, "Did you hear that there was a problem with the sound system?"

"No. Misha from Guest Services, said it was fine this morning. But she's off duty now."

"Where are those other workers? Tanya asked. After receiving blank stares, she explained what Harry had told her.

"I don't know who they'd be. We're the ones who set up the rooms."

Walking towards the access door to the stage, Harry said, "I'll take a look."

"You know electronics?" she asked.

"Are you kidding? I set up my grandson's Xbox and the rest of the rubbish that clutters up his room. All by myself."

Connections 8   THE GIFT OF TIME   Paul Stuart

Tanya understood enough to get by, but by the standards of youngsters today, she was a virtual luddite. She smiled indulgently and opened the door for him to descend into the gloom beneath the stage. A few minutes later the PA system came on with a resonant click through the speakers. She applauded his achievement.

"Those guys earlier knocked the wire loose when they were under there. We'll have to keep an eye out so they don't do it again. I think they're coming back," Harry said.

"Why do you think that?" asked Tanya.

"They left a toolbox and some bottles down there. Probably cleaner, I think." Harry answered.

"Okay, we'll keep an eye out," she said.

Her mind was already elsewhere, however. The decorations still had to be put up and food needed to be arranged. She wanted the room to be as nice as possible for the 200 or so people who'd been looking forward to the party for months.

A stroke of luck .....and good policing. Now two individuals were in custody. Emily was standing in a car park next to the sprawling Cribbs Causeway shopping complex. Mike O'Neil approached. He looked like a character from a John Steinbeck novel, perhaps Doc in Cannery Row. He was dressed in a jacket, blue shirt and wore no tie. His hair was salt and pepper and his brown eyes, beneath lids that dipped low, moved slowly as he explained the pursuit and arrest. His physique was solid and his arms were very strong, but not from spending time

Connections 8   THE GIFT OF TIME   Paul Stuart

in a gym. He was a fisherman and his strength came from fighting large sea creatures.

He was taciturn by design and his face rarely registered emotion, but with Emily he could usually be counted on to crack a wry joke or banter. Not now, though. Now he was all business.

A fellow officer, massive shaven-headed Albert Stemple, stalked up and O'Neil explained to him and Emily how individuals had been caught.

The fastest way out of the area was on the motorway north, which would take the suspected terrorists directly back to their Midland nest. That route was where the bulk of the searchers had been concentrating, with no success.

However, an inventive young officer had asked himself how he would leave the area, if he knew his mission was compromised. He decided that the smartest approach would be to lose himself amongst thick traffic, such as the many car parks at Cribbs Causeway, and then to use small neighbourhood roads out of the area, cross country, finally picking up the motorway many miles and hours away. The officer concentrated on this line of thinking, and eventually spotted the wanted car near the car park. After a ten-minute pursuit it vanished, but the officer decided they were trying a feint. He didn't head in the same direction. Instead he squealed to a stop and waited, hidden from view, in a side road.

After five excessively long and tense minutes, the wanted car sped the way it had come in, only to find the officer had anticipated them. He knew he

Connections 8   THE GIFT OF TIME   Paul Stuart

had to bring the car to a stop and didn't have time to wait for support, so he accelerated into his quarry and smashed into the driver's door. He was certain of at least detaining one of the two and that man was handcuffed almost before he drew breath. The other sprinted towards a warehouse area a few hundred yards away. He was trapped, but it took the dog support unit to persuade him that it was time to give up. The German Shepherd eventually, but reluctantly, released his grip on the man's arm, but not before he'd drawn blood and torn a good deal of flesh. The handler had been deliberately slow in giving his charge the release order and the dog had enjoyed a few extra moments of bloody pleasure.

"Nice day for an event," Vladimir Kirov said, as he tried to see what was happening to his accomplice, who was holding his arm at a peculiar angle. Kirov was a lean man; skinny you could say. Parentheses of creases surrounded his mouth, and his dark, narrow-set eyes hid beneath a severely straight fringe of black hair. He had a hook nose and long arms with big hands, but he didn't appear particularly strong.

Albert Stemple, whose every muscle seemed to be massive, stood nearby and eyed the prisoner carefully, ready to step on the bug if need be. O'Neil took a phone call. He stepped away.

Kirov repeated, "Event. Event. That could describe a game, you know." He spoke in an oddly high voice, which Emily found irritating. Probably not the tone, more the smirk with which the words

Connections 8   THE GIFT OF TIME   Paul Stuart

were delivered. "Or it could be a tragedy. Like they'd call an earthquake or a nuclear meltdown an 'event.' The media, I mean. They love words like that."

O'Neil motioned Emily aside.

"That was the station. It seems Kirov's on the Watch List. The other one, him with the bloody arm, is also on that list. Ladislav Tolkev, he's technical. Could be a bomb maker. He's probably the one who set it up."

"So, we're dealing with a possible bomb?"

"Don't know. There's no information about the means. The spooks have found their website and it talks about doing anything and everything to make their point. Biological, chemical, snipers, ISIS connections, maybe a joint venture."

Emily's mouth tightened. Her eyes took in Kirov, sitting on the kerb, and she noted that he was relaxed, even jovial. She approached him and regarded the lean man calmly. "We understand you're planning an attack of some sort."

"Event," he reminded her.

"Event, then. In two and a half hours. Is that true?"

"Indeed it is," he replied, smiling.

"Well, right now the only crimes you'll be charged with are traffic violations. At the worst, we could get you for conspiracy and attempt, several different counts. If that event occurs and people lose their lives…"

"The charges will be lot more serious," he said, jovially. "Let me ask you, what's your name?"

Connections 8   THE GIFT OF TIME   Paul Stuart

"You may call me Emily," she said, not bothering to show her ID card.

He smacked his lips. As irritating as his voice. "Well, Emily, if that's your name, let me ask you. Don't you think we have a few too many laws in this country? My goodness, Moses gave us ten. They seemed to work pretty well, but now our government tell us what to do about almost everything. And what not to do. Every little detail. Honestly! They don't have faith in our good, smart selves."

"Mr. Kirov.."

"Call me Vladimir, please."

He looked her over appraisingly and seemed to like what he saw. Emily was used to being undressed in the minds of interviewees, but this was different. He seemed to be pitying her, as if she were afflicted with a disease. In her case, she guessed, the disease was the tumour of government and its agencies. She noted the impervious smile on his face, his air of ....what? Yes, almost triumph. He didn't appear at all concerned about being arrested.

She glanced at her watch: 1:37. She stepped away to take a call on her mobile which updated her on the status of the other man. O'Neil tapped her on the shoulder and she followed his gaze.

Three black SUVs sped into the car park and squealed to a halt, lights flashing. At least six men climbed out and two dressed for warfare followed. The leader of the party strode forward.

"Hello, Steve." Emily knew him.

Connections 8   THE GIFT OF TIME   Paul Stuart

Stephen Nichols was the head of the local arm of MI5. He was a competent agent, but Emily thought he lacked ambition.

"I didn't get any details on this one," he said.

"Nor did we," Emily replied.

"Who's he?" Nichols asked.

Kirov stared back with amused hostility towards Nichols, who would represent that most pernicious of enemies: the government.

Emily explained his role and what he was believed to have done there.

"Any idea exactly what they have in mind?"

"Not so far," Emily said.

"There were two of them?" Nichols asked.

"Over there. His name's Ladislav Tolkev. I'm afraid the dog had a nice little chew on his arm, but he's ok. He'll live with a few stitches."

Nichols hesitated, looking at the fog coming in fast. "I've been sent to pick them up," Nichols said, wary of her reaction. His glance took in O'Neil as well, although he wasn't really bothered about him. It was Emily that worried Steve Nichols. She had a reputation for being feisty and clever. He had also heard on the grapevine that she had powerful connections. Not a woman to be crossed or upset.

Emily picked up his nervousness and understood it. She was pleased and smiled inwardly. She knew Nichols could not possibly know how powerful her connections really were. She also wondered whether this particular colleague had come across her beloved Books. She thought not,

Connections 8   THE GIFT OF TIME   Paul Stuart

because it would have been mentioned. Whispered in reverential and respectful tones. She felt the warm familiar glow as she thought about Books, and noted the moistness starting in certain places. He always had that effect. It was like magic. She didn't understand how he did it, but she loved every second.

Tearing herself away, she said, "We haven't got much time. How many people do you have?"

"Trained interrogators, you mean? Just me for now. I've been told there's somebody else on his way as well, but he won't be here for some time." Steve Nichols was not comfortable.

"Let's split them up," Emily suggested. "Give me one of them. At least for the time being, until you're up to strength."

Nichols was unsure. "I suppose."

Emily pressed on. "Kirov's going to be the trickiest. He's senior and not in the least bit shaken by being arrested." She nodded towards Kirov, who was relentlessly lecturing anybody who was within earshot about the destruction of the individual by the government "He's going to be trickier to break. Tolkev's been wounded and that'll make him more vulnerable. The dog has done us a favour at least. Might even be useful as a scare tactic. You never know."

She could see Nichols was considering her reasoning, but didn't wait for that process to run its natural, slow, course. "I think given our different

Connections 8   THE GIFT OF TIME   Paul Stuart

styles, background, yours and mine, it would make sense for me to take Kirov and you take Tolkev."

Nichols squinted against some momentary glare as a roll of fog vanished. "Who's Tolkev exactly?"

O'Neil answered, "Seems to be the technician. He'd know about the device, if that's what they've planted. Even if he doesn't tell you directly, he could give something away that'd let us figure out what's going on."

Nichols had noticed that O'Neil was supporting his female colleague and questions filled his mind. Did Emily's idea to split up the interrogation make sense? Did she and he actually have different styles and backgrounds? Would agreement to her plan later be taken as weakness and do his career plan some harm? Was she bluffing, hoping that she would get Tolkev if he insisted on the other way around? Or did her suggestion make absolute sense? He made a decision because he couldn't afford the time to stall or be seen to be weak and unsure. Emily knew all this and waited for him to catch up.

Finally, he nodded agreement and Kirov was escorted by Albert Stemple, none too gently, into Emily's presence.

"Do you know the five reasons the government is a travesty?" Kirov was winding up for a long lecture. "First, economically. I..."

Emily wanted to shut him up and was sorely tempted to practice her kick boxing skills by placing

Connections 8   THE GIFT OF TIME   Paul Stuart

her right foot forcibly on the left side of his jaw bone, just where it would crack, fracture and come loose. The memory of the satisfactory noise made by that move against another deserving person not that long ago, Ross was his name, almost made the urge irresistible.

Kirov was blissfully unaware of the imminent danger and was saved by Nichols who muttered, "whatever," and wandered off to await his own prisoner. Emily nodded and Stemple escorted Kirov to a car and inserted him in the back.

"Can you do the necessary?" she asked O'Neil.

"Of course," he replied and moved away to supervise the crime scene, canvass for witnesses and search for evidence, including anything that may have been thrown from the car.

As she got into her own, unmarked, car she called to Nichols and anybody else who was listening, "Remember, we have two and a half hours We have to move fast."

She turned on the flashing lights and left rubber on the concrete as she sped away.

It didn't take her long to get back, but Albert Stemple was already waiting, looking with some contempt at the press vans that loitered near the front door. Emily parked behind them and strode to him.

A reporter pushed forward and thrust a microphone their way.

"Emily! Emily!"

Connections 8   THE GIFT OF TIME   Paul Stuart

She knew the reporter. He was a sleazebag in her humble opinion. He oozed towards the tawdrier aspects of a story like slugs to her father's doomed vegetable garden. His cameraman, a squat froggy man with crinkly and unwashed hair, aimed a fancy Sony device their way as if he was about to launch a rocket propelled grenade.

"No comment about anything," she called as she and Stemple shoehorned Vladimir Kirov out of the car.

The reporter ignored her. "Can you give us your name?" This was aimed at the suspect.

Kirov was all too happy to talk. He began a lecture about how the fourth estate was in the pocket of big business and the government.

"Not all of us," the reporter called. "Not all of us. Keep talking Vladimir. We're with you!"

This impressed Kirov.

"You be quiet" Emily muttered, leading him towards the front door.

"And we're about to strike a blow for freedom!"

"What are you going to do, Vladimir?" The reporter shouted.

"We have no comment," Emily answered.

"Well, I do. I've only been arrested," Vladimir offered energetically, with a smile, ignoring Emily and pulling a face for the camera. "I'm not under any gagging order. Freedom of speech! That's what we believe in, even if these people in charge don't."

"Let him talk," the reporter said.

Connections 8   THE GIFT OF TIME   Paul Stuart

"We have no comment at the moment," Emily offered.

The reporter replied, "we don't want your comment, Emily. We want Vladimir's." Then he added, "were you hurt, Vladimir? You're limping."

"They hurt me in the arrest. That'll be part of the lawsuit."

He hadn't been limping earlier. Emily tried to keep the disgust off her face.

"We heard there were other suspects. One's wounded and in custody. The other's at large."

Police scanners. Emily grimaced. It was illegal to hack cell phones, but anybody could buy a scanner and learn all they wanted to about police operations.

"Vladimir, what do you expect to achieve by what you're doing?"

"Making the people aware of the overbearing government. The disrespect for the people of this country and...."

Emily actually pushed him through the door and into the building. She turned to him. "Vladimir, I've read you your rights, so I won't go through that again. OK?"

"No problem," he replied.

"Do you want to waive your right to a solicitor and to remain silent?"

"Yes."

"You understand that you can stop our interview at any time?"

Connections 8   THE GIFT OF TIME   Paul Stuart

"I didn't, but I do now. Thanks," Vladimir Kirov said.

"Will you tell us where you're planning this attack?" Do that and we could come to an arrangement."

"Will you let our leader go free? He's been illegally arrested."

"We can't do that."

"Then I think I'm not inclined to tell you what we've got in mind." A grin. "But I'm happy to talk. Always enjoy a good chinwag with an attractive woman."

Emily nodded to Stemple, who guided Kirov through the maze of hallways to an interrogation room. She followed and took the file that a colleague had put together on the suspect. Three pages were all it amounted to. Is that all, she wondered as she flipped open the file and read the sparse history of Vladimir Kirov and the pathetic organization he was sacrificing his life for.

She paused only once; to glance at her watch and learn that she had only two hours and one minute to stop the attack.

Connections 8   THE GIFT OF TIME   Paul Stuart

-3-

Michael O'Neil was pursuing the case at the crime scene, as he always did: meticulously, patiently. If an idea occurred to him, if a clue presented itself, he followed the lead until it paid off or it turned to dust.

He finished jotting down largely useless observations and impressions of witnesses in front of where the suspects' car had been rammed. The detective felt a coalescing of moisture on his face as the fog surrounded him. He wiped his face with broad palms. On the water, fishing from his boat, he didn't think anything of the damp air. Now, it was irritating.

He approached the head of the local forensics unit, Abbott Calderman. What parent on earth would have the vindictiveness to name a child 'Abbott'? he wondered. The Abbott's team was clustered around the still steaming car, practically dismantling it, to find clues that could tell them anything about the impending attack. Officers were also examining, then bagging and tagging, items from the pockets of the two suspects. Wallets, loose change, receipts, paper money (serial numbers, thanks to ATMs, revealed more than you'd think) sunglasses, keys and so on. These items would be examined for information about the event Vladimir Kirov had so proudly referred to.

Calderman was speaking to one of his people who was swathed in bright blue crime scene overalls, booties and a surgeon's shower cap.

Connections 8   THE GIFT OF TIME   Paul Stuart

"Michael, my people are going through the car." A glance at the smashed vehicle with its inflated air bags, only just getting wrinkled as they lost compression. "It's clean. No motel keys, letters or anything useful."

They hadn't really expected a map with a large red X and an arrow, but they had hoped.

"We'll know more when we analyse the trace from the tyres and the floor of the passenger compartment and the boot. But they did find a flask of coffee."

"Still hot?"

"Oh yes," Calderman nodded as he realised that O'Neil had caught the significance of the discovery. "And no receipts from Starbucks, Costa or anywhere else."

"So they might've stayed the night here somewhere and brewed it this morning."

"Possibly."

Finding the thermos suggested, though hardly proved, that they'd travelled a day or two early to prepare for the attack. This meant there'd probably be a motel nearby, with additional evidence. Though they'd been too smart to keep receipts or reservation records.

The Crime Scene officer added, "But most important. We found three cups inside. Two in the cup holders in the front, one on the floor in the back, and the rear floor was wet with spilled coffee."

"So, there's a third person?" O'Neil asked.

Connections 8   THE GIFT OF TIME   Paul Stuart

"Looks that way, though the officer who hit them didn't see anybody else. Could've been hiding in the back."

O'Neil considered this and made a phone call. He then texted Emily and let her know about the third suspect. He disconnected and looked over the hundred or so people standing at the police tape gawking at the activity.

The third one....maybe he'd got out of the car earlier, after setting up the attack but before the officer found the suspects. Or maybe he'd bailed out here, when their car was momentarily out of sight.

O'Neil summoned several officers and they headed behind the long building, searching the loading docks and the skips for any trace of a third suspect. He had hopes of success. Perhaps the suspect had bailed out because he had particularly sensitive or incriminating information on him. Or he was a local contact who did use credit cards and ATM machines, whose paper trail could steer the police towards the target. Or maybe he was the sort who couldn't resist interrogation. Perhaps even a child.

But the search team found no hint that someone had got out of the car and fled. The rear of the shopping centre faced a hill of sand, dotted with plants. The area was crowned with a tall chain link fence, topped with barbed wire. It would have been possible, though difficult, to escape that way, but there were no footprints in the sand leading to the fence. All the loading dock doors were locked and

Connections 8   THE GIFT OF TIME   Paul Stuart

alarmed, so he could not have gained entry that way.

O'Neil continued to the far side of the building. He walked there now and noted a Burger King about fifty or sixty feet away. He entered the restaurant, carefully scanning to see if anyone avoided eye contact, looked out of place or, more helpfully, took off quickly.

No one did. But that didn't mean the third suspect wasn't there. It happened relatively often. Not because of the adage (which was wrong) about returning to the scene of the crime out of a subconscious desire to get caught. No, criminals were often arrogant enough to stay around and scope out the nature of the investigation, as well as the identities of the investigators who were pursuing them, even, in some cases, taking digital images to let their friends know who was searching for them.

He interviewed the diners, asking if they'd seen anyone get out of the car behind the store. Typical of witnesses, people had seen two cars, three cars, red ones, and blue ones but no one had seen any passengers exit any vehicles. Finally, though, he had some luck. One woman nodded in answer to his questions. She pulled gaudy glasses out of her blond hair, where they rested like a tiara, and put them on, squinting as she looked over the scene thoughtfully. Pointing with her gigantic soda cup, she indicated a spot behind the stores where she'd noticed a man standing next to a car that could have been blue. She didn't know if he'd got out of the car

Connections 8   THE GIFT OF TIME   Paul Stuart

or not. She explained that somebody in the car handed him a blue backpack and he'd left. Her description of the men left no doubt that the men in the car were Kirov and Tolkev.

"Did you see where he went?"

"Towards the car park, I think. I, like, didn't pay much attention." Looking around. Then she stiffened. "Oh..."

"What?" O'Neil asked.

"That's him!" she whispered, pointing to a sandy haired man in jeans and work shirt, with a backpack over his shoulder. Even from this distance, O'Neil could see he was nervous, rocking from foot to foot, as he studied the crime scene. He was short which explained why he might easily have been missed in the back of the car.

O'Neil called for a uniformed officer to take the woman's particulars. She agreed to stay until they arrested the suspect so that she could make a formal ID.

"Oh, I almost forgot," the woman said, "that backpack? They handled it really carefully. I thought it had something breakable in, but now I think it might be dangerous."

"Thank you," said O'Neil, meaning it.

It was at that moment that the sandy haired man glanced towards him. And at that moment he understood. He eased back into the crowd. Shoving the backpack higher up on his shoulder, he turned and began to run, speeding between buildings to the back of the shopping centre. There he hesitated for

Connections 8   THE GIFT OF TIME   Paul Stuart

only a moment, charged up the sandy hill and scaled the six-foot chain-link fence that O'Neil had studied earlier. He shredded part of his jacket as he deftly vaulted the barbed wire. He sprawled onto the unkempt land on the other side of the fence, and lay there for a brief moment taking stock of his situation.

O'Neil and two uniformed officers approached the fence. The detective scaled it quickly, tearing his shirt and losing some skin on the back of his hand as he crested the barbed wire. He leapt down onto the waste ground, rolled once, righted himself and prepared for an attack.

The fugitive was nowhere to be seen.

One of the uniforms behind him got most of the way up the fence, but lost his grip and fell. He dropped straight down, off balance, and O'Neil heard the pop of his ankle as it broke.

"Oh," the young man muttered as he looked down at the odd angle. He turned as pale as the fog and passed out.

The other officer called for a medic and then started up the fence.

"No!" shouted O'Neil. "Stay there."

"But..."

"I'll handle the pursuit. Call for back up and the eye in the sky." O'Neil turned, sprinting across the waste ground.

He didn't want to do this alone but he had no choice. Just after he'd landed, he'd seen a sign laying face up.

Connections 8   THE GIFT OF TIME   Paul Stuart

DANGER
UNEXPLODED ORDANCE

The red lettering had faded and was now pink.

But O'Neil thought of the two hundred people who'd die in less than two hours and began to sprint along the trail that the suspect had been kind enough to leave in the wet ground. He knew, however, that he would not be able to outrun any explosion he might trigger, and that thought brought him no comfort at all.

Connections 8   THE GIFT OF TIME   Paul Stuart

-4-

Kinesic analysis works because of one simple concept, which Emily thought of as the Ten Commandments Principle. Although she herself was not religious, she liked the metaphor. It boiled down to simply: Thou Shalt Not.....

What came after that prohibition didn't matter. The gist was that people knew the difference between right and wrong and they felt uneasy doing something they shouldn't. Some of this is deceptive (either actively mis-stating or failing to give the whole story) they experience stress and this stress reveals itself. Charles Darwin said, "repressed emotion almost always comes to the surface in some form of body motion."

The problem for interrogators is that stress doesn't necessarily show up as nail biting, sweating and eye avoidance. It could take the form of a pleasant grin, a cheerful nod, a sympathetic wag of the head. What a body language expert must do is compare subjects' behaviour in non-stressful situations with their behaviour when they might be telling lies. Differences between the two suggest, though they don't prove, deception. If there is some variation, a kinesic analyst then continues to probe the topic that's causing the stress until the subject confesses, or it's otherwise explained.

In interrogating Vladimir Kirov, Emily would take her normal approach: asking a number of innocuous questions that she knew the answers to and the suspect would have no reason to lie about.

Connections 8   THE GIFT OF TIME   Paul Stuart

She'd also just shoot the breeze with him, no agenda other than to note how he behaved when feeling no stress. This would establish his kinesic 'baseline'; a catalogue of his body language, tone of voice and choice of expressions when he was at ease and truthful.

Only then would she turn to questions about the impending attack and look for variations from the baseline when he answered. But establishing the baseline usually requires many hours, if not days, of casual discussion.

Time that Emily did not have. It was now 2.08.

Still, there was no option other than to do the best she could. She'd learned that there was another suspect, escaping across waste ground, with Michael O'Neil in pursuit. Also, officers were still going over the car and the items that Tolkev and Kirov had on them when arrested. But these aspects of the investigation had produced no leads.

Emily now scanned the sparse file once more quickly. Vladimir Kirov was forty-four. He'd left school at the age of sixteen, but was now one of the 'philosophers' of the terrorist group. He wrote many of the essays and diatribes on the group's blog and website. He was single and had never married. He didn't have a passport and had never been out of the country. His father had been shot dead in a mishandled police raid some years ago and his mother and sister, both older than him, were also involved in the group. Neither of those family members had a criminal record.

Connections 8   THE GIFT OF TIME   Paul Stuart

Kirov, on the other hand, did, but it was a minor one and did not feature any violence. He also had an older brother who had not had any contact with the group, nor with Kirov for years. A deeper search had revealed nothing about Kirov's and Tolkev's journey to that point. This was typical because they paid cash for as much as they could.

Normally, she'd want far more details than this, but there was no more time.

Fast.

Emily left the folder at the front desk and entered the interrogation room. Kirov glanced up with a smile.

"Uncuff him," she said to Albert Stemple, who didn't hesitate even though he clearly wasn't keen on the idea.

Emily would be left alone in the room with an unshackled suspect, but she couldn't afford to have the man's arms limited by chains. Body language analysis is hard enough even with all limbs unfettered.

Kirov slumped lazily in the grey padded chair, as if settling in to watch a football match involving his favourite team. Emily nodded to Stemple, who left and closed the thick door behind him. Her eyes went to the large analogue clock at the far end of the room.

2.16.

Kirov followed her gaze, then looked back. "You're going to find out where the event's taking

Connections 8   THE GIFT OF TIME   Paul Stuart

place. Ask away. I'll tell you right now, you'll be wasting your time."

Emily moved her chair so that she sat across from him, with no furniture between them. Any barrier between interviewer and subject, even a small table, gives the suspect a sense of protection and makes body analysis that much harder. Emily was about three feet from him, in his personal space, not close enough to make him stonewall, but near enough to unsettle him.

Except that he wasn't unsettled at all. He was as calm as could be. He looked at her steadily, a gaze that was not haughty, not challenging, not sexy. It was as if he were sizing up a dog to buy for his child.

"Vladimir, you haven't got a driving licence."

"Don't want one and don't need one. The less the powers that be know about you, the better."

"Where do you live?" she asked.

"You know that already," he replied. "Your trying to establish contact, gain trust, set a baseline. Waste of time. In fact, it's patronising and insulting." Vladimir was pleased with himself.

Emily nevertheless pressed on and asked more about his personal life and travels, pretending not to know the answers. She'd left the file outside deliberately.

He played along, knowing it was using time. Her time. Not his. As he spoke she noted his shoulders were forward, his right hand tended to come to rest on his thigh, he looked her straight in

Connections 8   THE GIFT OF TIME   Paul Stuart

the eye when he spoke and his lips often curled into a half smile. He had a habit of poking his tongue into the interior of his cheek from time to time. It could have been a habit or could be from some withdrawal, such as smoking or chewing something.

"Why did you come here, Vladimir?" Emily asked.

"Don't know, really," he replied. I've noticed the weather's not much to write home about," he quipped.

"That's true," she said.

He beamed in an eerie way.

"I like you," he said. "You're a firecracker, Emily."

A chill coursed down her spine as the near set eyes tapped across her face. She ignored it as best as she could and asked, "How senior are you in your organisation?"

"Pretty near the top," he couldn't help bragging. "Do you know anything about us?"

"No," Emily lied.

"I'd love to tell you. You're smart, Mrs Firecracker. I bet you'd agree with some of our ideas." He was taunting her now.

"I'm not sure I would," she answered.

He gave a one shouldered shrug, which was another of his baseline gestures. "Oh, you never know. You might surprise yourself," he said.

Emily continued with more questions. She knew the answers to some, but the others were such that he'd have no reason to lie and she continued to

Connections 8   THE GIFT OF TIME   Paul Stuart

rack up elements of baseline body language and the tone and speed of his speech.

She risked a glance at the clock.

"You're worried about time, aren't you?" Kirov asked rhetorically.

"You're planning to kill a lot of people. Yes, that bothers me. But not you, I notice."

"Ha, now you're sounding just like a therapist. I was in counselling once. It didn't work." Kirov was enjoying himself.

"Let's talk about what you have planned; the two hundred people you are going to kill." Emily wanted progress.

"Two hundred and more probably," he said.

"How many more?"

"Two twenty, I'd say," he replied.

So, more victims. His behaviour fitted the baseline. This was true; he wasn't just boasting.

An idea occurred to Emily and she said, "I've told you we're not releasing your leader. That will never be on the table."

Your loss. Well, not yours. Two hundred and some odd people." Vladimir said.

"Killing them will only make your organisation a pariah, a ..."

"I know what a pariah means. Go on."

"Don't you think it would work to your advantage, from a publicity point of view, if you call off the attack, or tell me the location now?" Emily pressed.

Connections 8   THE GIFT OF TIME   Paul Stuart

Kirov hesitated. "Maybe. That could be." Then his eyes brightened. "I'm not inclined to call anything off. That'd look bad. Or tell you where this thing's going to happen. But, as I like you, how about I give you a chance to figure it out. We'll play a game."

"Game?" she asked.

"Twenty questions. I'll answer honestly, I promise. If you find out where those two hundred and twenty souls are going to meet Jesus, then good for you. I can honestly say I didn't tell you. But you only get twenty questions. You don't figure it out, then get the coffins ready. You want to play, Emily? If not, I'll just decide I want my legal rights and hope I'm next to a TV in one hour and forty-one minutes." He had looked at the clock on the wall.

"All right," Emily said. "Let's play." She subtly wiped the sweat that had dotted her palms. How on earth to frame twenty questions to narrow down where the attack would take place?

He sat forward. "This'll be fun."

"Is the attack going to be an explosive device?"

"Question one. No. I'll keep count, if you like," he volunteered brightly.

"What will it be?"

"That's question two. Sorry, you know the rules. It has to be yes or no answers. But I'll be generous and give you that for free."

"Will it be a chemical/biological weapon?" she asked.

Connections 8 THE GIFT OF TIME Paul Stuart

"Now you're cheating," he teased. "That's sort of two questions, but I'll say yes."

"Is it going to be in a place open to the public?"

"Number three. Yes, sort of. Let's say there'll be public access."

He was telling the truth. All his behaviour and the pitch and tempo of his voice bore out his honesty. But what did he mean by public access but not quite public?

"Is it an entertainment venue?"

"Question four. Well, not really, but there will be entertainment there."

"Christmas related?"

He scoffed. "That's five. Are you asking questions wisely, little Miss Firecracker? You've used a quarter up already. You could have combined Christmas and entertainment. Anyway, yes, Christmas is involved."

Emily thought this curious. The group reportedly had a religiously side, even if they weren't born again fanatics. She would have thought the target might be Islamic or Jewish.

"Have the victims done anything to your organisation personally?" She was thinking of government or law enforcement.

"Six. No."

"You're targeting them on ideological grounds?"

"Seven. Yes."

"Will it be here, in this area?"

Connections 8   THE GIFT OF TIME   Paul Stuart

"Number eight. Yes."

"Will it be near the water?"

"Sloppy question. I expect better from you. I'll let you have that for free."

Stupid of her, Emily realised, her heart pounding. There were a number of bodies of water and rivers in the area. She spotted that he hadn't actually answered that question, though.

"Will it be within half a mile of where we arrested you?"

"Good! Much better!" he said, enjoying himself. "Yes. That was nine. Almost halfway there."

She could see he was telling the truth completely. Every answer was delivered according to his baseline.

"Do you and Ladislav Tolkev have a partner helping you in the event?

One eyebrow rose. "Yes. Number ten. You're halfway to saving all those poor people, Emily."

"Is this third person a member of your organisation?"

"Yes. Eleven."

She was thinking hard, unsure how to finesse the partner's existence into helpful information. She changed tack. "Do the victims need tickets to get into the venue?"

"Twelve. I want to play fair. I honestly don't know. But they did have to sign and pay. That's more than I should give, but I'm enjoying this."

She was beginning to form some ideas.

"Is the venue a tourist attraction?"

Connections 8   THE GIFT OF TIME   Paul Stuart

"Thirteen. Yes, I'd say so. At least near tourist attractions."

Now she felt safe using one of her geographical questions. "Is it in Bristol?"

"No. Fourteen."

"Plymouth?"

"No. Fifteen."

Emily kept her own face neutral. What else should she be asking? If she could narrow it down a bit more, and if Michael O'Neil and his team came up with other details, they might cobble together a clear picture of where the attack would take place and then evacuate every building in the area.

"How are you doing there, Emily? Feeling the excitement of a good game? I am." He looked at the clock. Emily did, too. Hell, time had sped by during this exchange. It was now 2.42

She didn't respond to his question, but tried a different tack. "Do your close friends know what you're doing?"

He frowned. "You want to use question sixteen for that? Well, your choice. Yes."

"Do they approve?"

"Yes, all of them. Seventeen. Getting all you need here, Emily? Seems to me you're getting off the track."

But she wasn't. Emily had another strategy. She was comfortable with the information she had. Tourist area, near the water, a paid for event, Christmas related, a few other facts. Put all that together with what O'Neil found, she hoped they

Connections 8 THE GIFT OF TIME Paul Stuart

could narrow down areas to evacuate. Now she was hoping to convince him to confess by playing up the idea raised earlier. That by averting the attack he'd still score some good publicity but wouldn't have to go to jail forever. Even if she lost the Twenty Questions game, which seemed likely, she was getting him to think about the people he was close to, friends and family he could still spend time with if he stopped the attack.

"And family? Do your siblings approve?"

"Question eighteen. Don't have any. I'm an only child. You only got two questions left, Emily. Spend them wisely.

Emily hardly heard the last sentences. She was stunned. His behaviour when he'd made the comment about not having siblings, which was a lie, was identical to that of the baseline. During the entire game he had not been telling the truth.

Their eyes met. "Tripped up there, didn't I?" He laughed hard. "We're off the grid so much, didn't think you knew about my family. Should've been more careful."

"Everything you told me was a lie."

"Thin air. Smoke and mirrors. Pick your cliché, Emily. Had to run the clock. There's nothing on God's green earth going to save those people."

"She understood now what a waste of time this had been. Vladimir Kirov was probably incapable of being kinesically analysed. The Ten Commandments Principle didn't apply in his case. Kirov felt no more stress telling lies than he did telling the truth. Like serial killers and schizophrenics, political extremists often feel they are doing what's right, even if those acts are criminal or reprehensible to others. They are convinced of their own moral rectitude.

"Look at it from my perspective. Sure, we would have got some media coverage if I'd confessed. But you know what they're like, those parasites would get tired of the story after a couple of days. Two hundred dead people? Hell, we'll be on mainstream news for weeks. You can't buy publicity like that."

Emily pushed back from the table and, without a word, stepped outside.

Connections 8   THE GIFT OF TIME   Paul Stuart

-5-

Michael O'Neil sprinted, gasping and sweating despite the chill and mist. He slowed gradually and jogged past car parks and skull and crossbones signs warning of unexploded ordnance. The suspect wove through the area desperately and the chase was exhausting. The land had been bulldozed at some time in history, but mounds of sand, some four stories high, remained. The fugitive made his way through these valleys in a panicked run, falling often, as did O'Neil because of the slippery surfaces. O'Neil debated using his Taser if the opportunity arose, but decided against it because of what might be in that backpack.

The fugitive chugged along, gasping, red-faced, the deadly backpack over his shoulder bouncing.

Finally, O'Neil heard the thud thud of rotors moving in. He reflected that a helicopter was the only smart way to pursue somebody through such an area. It wouldn't trigger the explosives as long it hovered above ground. Besides, what were the odds that he himself would detonate some ordnance, mangling his legs?

The chopper moved closer. God, it was loud. He'd forgotten just how loud. The suspect stopped, glance back and then turned right, disappearing behind a hill.

Was it a trap? O'Neil started forward slowly. But he couldn't see clearly. The chopper was raising a turbulent cloud of dust and sand. O'Neil waved it back. He pointed ahead of him and began to

Connections 8   THE GIFT OF TIME   Paul Stuart

approach the valley down which the suspect had disappeared.

The helicopter hovered closer yet. The pilot apparently hadn't seen O'Neil's hand gestures. The sandstorm grew fiercer. Some completely indiscernible words rattled from a loudspeaker.

"Back, back!" O'Neil called, uselessly.

Then, in front of him, he noticed what seemed to be a person's form, indistinct in the miasmic storm of dust and sand. The figure was moving in.

"Halt!" he called at the top of his voice.

He crouched and staggered forward. Damn chopper! Grit clotted his mouth. That was when a second silhouette, smaller, detached from the first and seemed to fly through the gauzy air towards him. The backpack struck him in the face. He fell backward, tumbling to the ground, the bag coming to rest beside his legs. Choking on sand, O'Neil thought how ironic it was that he'd survived a minefield only to be blown to pieces by a bomb the suspect had brought with him.

Connections 8   THE GIFT OF TIME   Paul Stuart

-6-

The Business Association holiday party was under way. It had started, as they always did, a little early. Who wanted to deny loans or take care of the massive paperwork of approved ones when the joy of the season beckoned?

The members were being greeted at the door, being shown where to hang their coats, accepting gift bags, drinks and nibbles. The place looked magical. Tanya had opted to close the curtains to close out the gloomy fog. The room had taken on a warm, comfy tone due to the holiday lights and dimmed overheads.

Harry was walking around in his conservative suit, white shirt and oversized Santa hat. People sipped wine and punch, snapped digital pictures and clustered, talking about politics and sports and shopping and impending holidays. Also, a lot of comments about interest rates, the Euro and Brexit. With bankers, you couldn't get away from shop talk. Ever.

"We heard there's a surprise, Tanya," somebody called.

"What?" came another voice.

"Be patient," she said laughing. "If I told you, it wouldn't be a surprise now, would it?"

When the party seemed to be spinning along on its own, she walked to the stage and tested the PA system once again. Yes, it was working fine. Thank goodness. The surprise depended on it. She'd arranged for the chorus from one of her grandsons'

Connections 8   THE GIFT OF TIME   Paul Stuart

schools to go onstage and present a holiday concert. She glanced at her watch. The kids would arrive at about 3.45. She'd heard the youngsters before and they were very good.

Tanya laughed to herself, recalling the entertainment at last year's party. Herb Ross, a Vice President at a well- known bank, who'd ingested close to a quart of the special punch, had climbed on the table to sing and to act out the entire 'Twelve Days of Christmas" himself, the leaping lords being the high point.

Emily spent a precious ten minutes texting and talking to a number of people in the field and at the station.

It seemed that outside the surreality of the interrogation room, the investigation hadn't moved well at all. The forensics unit was still analyzing material connected with the car and items from the suspects' pockets. Abbott Calderman said they might not have any answers for another ten or fifteen minutes.

Michael O'Neil, when last heard from, had been pursuing the third suspect. A police helicopter had lost him in a cloud of dust and sand. She'd had a brief conversation with Steve Nichols, who'd said, "This Tolkev isn't saying anything. Not a word. Just stares at me. We need to try something else."

Emily thought of Books. Perhaps it was time for these people to be introduced to her lovely Books.

She returned to Vladimir Kirov in the interrogation room. She looked at the clock on the wall.

3.10

"Hey," said Kirov, eying it briefly, then turning his attention to Emily. "You're not mad at me, are you?"

Emily sat across the table from him. It was clear she wasn't going to force a confession out of him, so she didn't bother with the tradecraft of kinesic interviewing.

Connections 8   THE GIFT OF TIME   Paul Stuart

"I'm sure it's no surprise that, before, I tried to analyse your body language and was hoping to come up with a way to pressure you into telling me what you and Ladislav and your other friend had planned," she said.

"Didn't know that about the body language. But it makes sense."

"Now I want to do something else, and I'm going to tell exactly what that is. No tricks."

"Fine. Whatever. It's your time to waste." Kirov was confident.

Emily had decided that traditional analysis and interrogation wouldn't work with someone like Vladimir Kirov. His lack of affect, his fanatic belief in the righteousness of his cause made kinesics useless. Content based analysis wouldn't do much good either; this is body language's poor cousin, seeking to learn whether a suspect is telling the truth by considering if what he says makes sense. But Kirov was too much in control to let slip anything that might pass for clues about deception and truth.

So she was doing something radical.

Emily now said, "I want to prove to you that your beliefs, what's motivating you and your group to perform this attack, are wrong."

He lifted an eyebrow. Intrigued.

This was a ludicrous idea for an interrogator. One should never argue substance with a suspect. If a man is accused of killing his wife, your job is to determine the facts and, if it appears that he did

Connections 8   THE GIFT OF TIME   Paul Stuart

indeed commit murder, get a confession or at least gather enough information to help investigators secure his conviction.

There's no point in discussing the right or wrong of what he did, much less the broader philosophical questions of taking lives in general or violence against women, say.

But that was exactly what she was going to do now. Poking the inside of his cheek with his tongue once more, thoughtful, Kirov said, "do you even know what our beliefs are?"

"I looked at your website."

"You like the graphics? Cost a pretty penny." Kirov smiled.

A glance at the wall. 3.14

Emily continued. "You advocate smaller government, virtually no taxes, decentralized banking, no large corporations, reduced military, religion in schools. And, that you have the right to violent civil disobedience. Along with some racial and ethnic theories that went out of fashion long, long ago."

"Well, about that last one. Truth is, we just throw that in to get hits on the site from right wing radicals and border control nuts. Lots of don't really feel that way. But, I must say, it seems that you've done your homework. We've got more positions than you can shake a stick at but those'll do for a start. So, argue away. This is going to be fun; I'm going to enjoy this. Just remember, though, maybe I'll talk you into my way of thinking, giving up that job of

Connections 8 THE GIFT OF TIME Paul Stuart

yours and coming over to the good guys. What do you think about that?" Kirov ended his speech and sighed with contentment.

Emily was also content, but the reason was different. She knew who she was working for, even though very few people actually did. She wasn't a police officer; she belonged to an elite group, begun by the now retired Ray Quinn, taken on by her father, Frank, and sanctioned at the highest level by the Prime Minister alone. And then there was Books. Her beloved Books. There was always the option of introducing Kirov to Books. She wondered if he still had his bolt cutters kicking around somewhere.

"I'll stay open-minded, if you will," Emily replied.

"Deal."

She thought back to what she'd read on the group's website. "You talk about the righteousness of the individual. Agree up to a point, but we can't survive as individuals alone. We need government. And the more people we have, with more social and economic activity, the more we need a strong central government to make sure we're safe to go about our lives."

"That's sad, Emily."

"Sad?"

"Sure. It sounds like I have more faith in humankind than you do. We're pretty capable of taking care of ourselves. Let me ask you. Do you go to the doctor from time to time?"

"Yes."

Connections 8   THE GIFT OF TIME   Paul Stuart

"But not very often, right? Pretty rare? More often with the kids, I'll bet. Sure, you have kids. I can tell."

She let this go with no reaction.

3.17

"But what does the doctor do? Short of broken bone to set, the doctor tells you pretty much to do what your instinct told you to do anyway. Take some aspirin, go to bed, drink plenty of fluids, eat fibre, go to sleep. Let the body take care of itself. And ninety per cent of the time, those ideas work." His eyes lit up. "That's what government should do. Leave us alone ninety per cent of the time."

"What about the other ten per cent," Emily queried.

"I'll give you what you need. Let's see: roads, airports, security, defence. Ah, but what's that last word? 'Defence?' Should really be called the War Office, but that doesn't sound good, does it? So they call it the Ministry of Defence. But that's a lie because it's not just defence. We go poking our noses into places that we have no business being."

"The government regulates companies that might exploit people."

He scoffed. "The government helps them do it. How many politicians go to London and come back rich? Most of them."

"But you're okay with some taxes."

He shrugged. "To pay for roads, air traffic control and defence."

3.20.

Connections 8   THE GIFT OF TIME   Paul Stuart

"The stock Exchange?"

"We don't need that. Ask your average man in the street what the stock market is and he'll say it's a way to make money or put something away for retirement. They don't realise that's what it's not for. The stock market is there to let people buy a company, like you go to buy a used car. And, why do you want to buy a company? Beats me. Maybe a few people buy shares because they like what the company does or they want to support a certain kind of business. That's not what people want them for. Do away with them. Live off the land."

"You're wrong, Vladimir. Look at all the innovations companies have created: the lifesaving drugs, the medical supplies, the computers....."

"Sure, and iPhones and laptops that have replaced parents, and children learn their family values at porn sites."

"What about the government providing education?"

"Ha! That's another racket. Professors make a few thousand pounds a year for working eight months, and not working very hard at that. Tell me, Emily, are you happy handing over your youngsters to somebody you see at one or two PTA meetings a year? Who knows what the hell they're poisoning their minds with? Home schooling is what I say."

"You don't like the police, you claim. But we're here to make sure you and your family are safe."

"Police state. Think on this, Emily. I don't know what you do exactly here, but tell me honestly.

Connections 8   THE GIFT OF TIME   Paul Stuart

You put your life on the line every day and for what? Oh, maybe you stop some crazy serial killer from time to time or save somebody in a kidnapping. But mostly police officers just put on their fancy uniforms and arrest some poor kids with drugs, but never get to the why of it. What's the reason they were scoring pot or sniffing coke in the first place? Because the government and the institutions of this country failed them."

3.26

"So you don't like the government. But it's all relative isn't it? Go back in history. We weren't just a mass of individuals. There was local government, under whatever label you care to put on it, and it was powerful. People had to pay taxes, they were subject to laws, they couldn't take their neighbour's property, they couldn't commit incest, they couldn't steal. Everybody accepted that. Today's government is just a bigger version."

"That's good, Emily. I'll give you that." He nodded agreeably. "But we think national and even local laws are too much."

"So you're in favour of no laws?"

"Let's just say a lot, lot less."

Emily leaned forward, with her hands together. "Then let's talk about your one belief that's the most critical now: violence to achieve your ends. I'll grant you that you have the right to hold whatever beliefs you want, and not get arrested for it. Which by the way, isn't true in a lot of countries."

Connections 8   THE GIFT OF TIME   Paul Stuart

"We're the best," Kirov agreed. "But that's still not good enough for us."

"But violence is hypocritical."

He frowned at this. "How so?"

"Because you take away the most important right of an individual; his life, when you kill him in the name of your views. How can you be an advocate of individuals and yet be willing to destroy them at the same time?"

His head bobbed up and down. A tongue poke again. "That's good, Emily. Yes."

She lifted her eyebrows.

Kirov added, "and there's something to it. Except you're missing one thing. Those people we're targeting? They're not individuals. They're part of the system, just like you."

"So your saying it's okay to kill them because they're, what? Not even human?"

"Couldn't have said it better myself, Emily." His eyes strayed to the wall. 3.34.

-8-

The helicopter set down in a car park and Michael O'Neil and a handcuffed suspect climbed out.

O'Neil was bleeding from a minor cut on the head incurred when he scrabbled into a cluster of prickly bushes escaping the satchel bomb.

Which turned out to be merely a distraction.

No IEDs, no anthrax.

The satchel was filled with sand.

The suspect had apparently disposed of whatever noxious substance it contained on one of his turns and weaves, and the evidence or bomb or other clue was lost in the sand.

The downdraft from the helicopter hadn't helped either.

What was most disappointing, though, was that the man had clammed up completely. O'Neil was wondering if he was actually mute. He hadn't said a word during the chase or after he had been tackled, handcuffed and dragged to the helicopter. Nothing O'Neil could say, promises or threats, could get the man to talk.

The man was processed. A fast search revealed no ID and his fingerprints did not trigger any recognition from the hand held scanner. The blond woman who had spotted him in the crowd now identified him formally and left. The Crime Scene Team Leader strode up to O'Neil.

"Don't have much, but I'd say the car recently spent some time on or near a beach."

Connections 8   THE GIFT OF TIME   Paul Stuart

Calderman explained that because of the unique nature of cooling water from the nearby power plant, and the prevailing currents and fertilizer from some of the local farms, he could pinpoint a part of the country to within five miles. If five miles could be called pinpointing.

"Anything else?"

"No. That's it. Might get more in the lab." Calderman nodded to his watch, "but there's no time left."

O'Neil called Emily, whose mobile phone went straight to voice mail. He texted the information. He then looked over at the smashed car, the emergency vehicles, the police tape stark in the foggy afternoon. He knew it wasn't unheard of for crime scenes to raise more questions than answers. But why did it have to be this one, when so little time remained to save the two hundred victims?

Connections 8   THE GIFT OF TIME   Paul Stuart

-9-

Hands steady as a rock, Harriet Kirov was driving the car she'd stolen from the car park at the shopping centre. But even as her grip was firm, her heart was in turmoil. Her beloved brother, Vladimir and her sometime lover, Ladislav Tolkev, were in custody. After the bomb detonated shortly, she'd never see them again, except at the trial. Given Vladimir's courage, she suspected he'd plead not guilty simply to be able to get up in court and give the judge and press an earful.

She pulled her glasses out of her hair and regarded her watch. Not long now. It was ten minutes to the Premier Inn, which had been their staging area. And would have been where they'd wait out the next few days, watching the news. But now, sadly, Plan B was in effect. She'd go back to collect all the documents, maps, extra equipment and remaining explosives and get the hell back home. She believed there had to be an informer there and she was going to find him.

It was a good thing they'd decided to split up behind the shops. As the car had temporarily evaded the patrol officer and skidded to a stop, Harriet in the backseat, Vladimir decided they had to make sure somebody got back to the motel and ditch the evidence, which implicated some very senior people in their organization.

She jumped out with the backpack containing extra detonators and wires and tools and phony IDs that let them get into the banquet hall. Harriet had

Connections 8   THE GIFT OF TIME   Paul Stuart

been going back to hijack a car and head back to the Premier Inn, but the officer had rammed Ladislav and Vladimir and then the police had descended.

She'd slipped into a Burger King to let the dust settle. She'd ditched the contents of the pack but, to her dismay, the police were spreading out and talking to everybody at the shopping centre. Harriet decided she had to find a fall guy to take attention away from her. She'd spotted a lone shopper, a man about her height with light hair, in case the officer had seen her in the backseat. She stuck her pistol in his ribs, pulled him behind the Burger King, and grabbed his wallet. She found a picture of three spectacularly plain children and make a fake call on her mobile to an imaginary assistant, telling him to go to the poor guy's house and round up the kids.

If he didn't do exactly as she said, they'd be shot, oldest youngest and his wife would watch and then be the last to go. She got his car keys and told him to stand in the crowd. If any police officers came to talk to him he was to run and, if he was caught, he should throw the pack at them and keep running. If he got stopped he should say nothing. She, of course, was going to identify him to the police and then take his car and leave when they went after him.

It would have worked except that O'Neil had made her stay put so she could formally identify the sandy haired man. She was desperate to get the hell out of there, but she couldn't arouse suspicion, so

Connections 8   THE GIFT OF TIME   Paul Stuart

Harriet had cooled her heels, sipping on her Diet Coke, trying to wrestle with the anger and sorrow about her brother and Gabe.

Then O'Neil and the poor man had returned. She'd identified him with a fierce glance of warning and given them some fake information on how to reach her. Now she was in his car, heading back to the Premier Inn. The motel loomed. She sped into the parking area and braked to a stop.

She was aware of an odd vibration under her hands. The steering column. What was it? An earthquake? A problem with the car? She turned the engine off, but the vibration grew louder. Leaves began to move and dust swirled like a tornado.

And Harriet understood. "Oh, shit."

She pulled her Glock from her bag and sprinted toward the motel door, firing blindly at the helicopter as it landed. Several officers and, damn it, that detective, O'Neil, charged towards her.

"Drop the weapon! Drop the weapon now!"

She hesitated and laid her gun and her keychain on the ground. Then she dropped facedown beside them. She was handcuffed and pulled to her feet.

O'Neil was approaching, his weapon drawn, looking for accomplices. A cluster of officers was slowly moving towards the motel room.

"Anyone in there?" he asked.

"No."

"It was just the three of you?"

"Yes."

Connections 8   THE GIFT OF TIME   Paul Stuart

The detective called, "Treat it dynamic in any case."

"How'd you know?" she snapped.

He looked her over neutrally. "The cargo pants."

"What?"

"You described the man in the car and said one was wearing cargo pants. You couldn't see the pants of somebody inside a car from sixty feet away. The angle was wrong."

Hell, Harriett thought. Never even occurred to her.

O'Neil added that the man they'd believed was one of the conspirators was acting too nervous. "It occurred to me that he might've been set up. He told me what you'd done. We tracked his car here with his GPS." O'Neil was going through her purse. "You're his sister, Vladimir's."

"I'm not saying anything else." Harriett was distracted, her eyes taking in the motel room.

O'Neil caught it and frowned. He glanced for at her keychain, which held both a fob for her car and the second one. She caught his eye and smiled.

"IED in the room!" he called. "Everybody back! Now."

It wasn't an explosive device, just a gas bomb Ladislav had rigged in the event that something like this happened. It had been burning for three minutes or so. She'd pushed the remote control the second she'd seen the chopper, but the smoke and flames weren't yet visible.

Connections 8   THE GIFT OF TIME   Paul Stuart

Then a bubble of fire burst through two of the windows. Armed with extinguishers, the tactical team hurried to salvage what they could, then retreated as the flames swelled. One officer called, "Michael! We spotted a box of plastic explosive detonators, some timers."

Another officer ran up to O'Neil and showed him what was left of a dozen scorched documents. They were the floor plan for the site of the CCCBA party. He studied it.   "A room with a stage. Could be anywhere. A corporation, school, hotel, restaurant." He sighed.

Harriett panicked, then relaxed, as she snuck a glimpse and noted that the name of the motel was on a part of the sheet that had burned to ash.

"Where is this?" O'Neil asked her bluntly.

Harriett studied it for a moment and shook her head.

"I've never seen that before. You planted it to incriminate me. You people do it all the time."

*

At the Bankers' party the children arrived, looking scrubbed and festive, all in uniforms. They were checking out the treats, and the boys were probably wondering if they could cop a spiked punch, but would refrain until after the twenty-minute concert. The kids took their music seriously and sweets tended to clog the throat. The call came for

Connections 8   **THE GIFT OF TIME**   Paul Stuart

everybody to take their seats and the children climbed up on stage, taking their positions.

*

The clock in the interrogation room registered 3:51. Emily broke off the debate for a moment and read and sent several text messages, as Vladimir Kirov watched with interest.
3:52
"Your expression tells me the news isn't good. Not making much headway elsewhere?"
Emily did not respond. She slipped her phone away.
"I'm not finished with our discussion, Vladimir. Now, I pointed out you were hypocritical to kill the very people you purport to represent."
"And I pointed out a hole a mile wide with that argument."
"Killing also goes against another tenet of yours."
Vladimir Kirov said calmly, "How so?"
"You want religion taught in school. So you must be devout. Well, killing the innocent is a sin."
He snickered. "Oh, please. Read the Bible sometime. Educate yourself. God smites people for next to nothing. Because somebody crosses Him or to get your attention. Or because it's Tuesday, I don't know. You think everybody drowned in Noah's flood was guilty of something?"

Connections 8   THE GIFT OF TIME   Paul Stuart

"So al-Qaeda terrorists are okay? What about Daesh? ISIS?"

"Well, al-Qaeda itself want the strongest government of all. It's called a theocracy. No respect for individuals. But their tactics? Hell, yes. I admire the suicide bombers. If I was in charge, though, I'd reduce all Islamic countries to smoking nuclear craters."

Emily looked desperately at the clock, which showed nearly 3:57. She rubbed her face as her shoulders slumped. Her weary eyes pleaded.

"Is there anything I can say to talk you into stopping this?"

3:58.

"No, you can't. Sometimes the truth is more important than the individuals. But," he added with a sincere look, "Emily, I want to say that I appreciate one thing."

"What's that?" she said in a whisper, eyes on the clock.

"You took me seriously. That talk we just had. You disagree, but you treated me with respect."

4:00.

Both Emily and her suspect remained motionless, staring at the clock. A phone in the room rang. She leaned over and pushed the speaker button. "Yes?"

The voice was full of static. "Emily, It's Albert. I'm sorry to have to tell you..."

She sighed, "go on."

Connections 8   THE GIFT OF TIME   Paul Stuart

"It was an IED. Plastic of some sort. We don't have the count yet. Wasn't as bad as it could be. Seems the device was under a stage and that absorbed some of the blast. But we're still looking at fifteen or so dead, maybe fifty injured. Hold on I'm wanted. I'll get back to you."

Emily disconnected, closed her eyes briefly then glared at Kirov. "How could you?"

Vladimir frowned; he wasn't particularly triumphant.

"I'm sorry, Emily. This is the way it had to be. It's a war out there. Besides score one for your side. Only fifteen dead. We screwed up."

Emily shivered in anger, but recovered sufficient composure to say, "let's go."

She rose and knocked on the door. It opened immediately and two large officers came in, also glaring. One pulled Kirov's hands roughly in front of him and snapped the handcuffs around his wrists as tightly as he could manage. He was hoping for a reaction, but Vladimir bit his lip and said nothing. The other officer was the epitome of decorum.

"Just heard, the death count's up to..."

She waved him silent, as if to deny Kirov the satisfaction of knowing the extent of his victory. She led the prisoner out of the back of the building towards a van that would ultimately take him to a cell.

"We have to move fast," she told the others. "There're going to be a lot of people who'd like to take things into their own hands."

Connections 8   THE GIFT OF TIME   Paul Stuart

The area was largely deserted. But just then the media scrum began.

"Emily," one reporter called, "could you comment on the failure of law enforcement to stop the bombing in time?"

She said nothing and kept ushering Kirov towards the van.

"Do you think this will be the end of your career?"

Silence.

"Vladimir, do you have anything to say?" the reporter asked.

Eyes on the camera lens, Kirov called, "it's about time the government started listening. This would never have happened if illegal arrests stopped."

"Vladimir, what do you have to say about killing innocent victims?"

"Sacrifices have to be made," he called.

"But why these particular people? What's the message you're trying to send?"

"That maybe bankers shouldn't be throwing themselves fancy holiday parties with the money they've stolen from the working people of this country. The finance industry's been raping citizens for years. They claim..."

"Okay. That's enough." Emily snapped to the officers flanking Kirov, who literally jerked him to stop. She pulled out a mobile. "Michael, it's Emily."

"We've got six choppers and the entire communications network standing by. You're

Connections 8   THE GIFT OF TIME   Paul Stuart

patched in to all emergency frequencies. What do you have?"

"The target's a party. Christmas I'd guess, involving bankers. It is a bomb and it's under the stage in that room you texted me about."

Vladimir Kirov stared at her, awash in confusion, as a torrent of voices answered.

"What is this?" Kirov raged.

Everyone ignored him.

A long several minutes passed, with Emily standing motionless, head down, listening to the intersecting voices. And then: "This is Major Rodriguez. We've got it. Bankers' Association annual Christmas party., They're evacuating now."

Vladimir Kirov's eyes grew wide as they stared at Emily. "But the bomb..." He glanced at Emily's wrist and those of the other officers. They'd all removed their watches, so Kirov couldn't see the real time. He turned to an officer and snapped, "what the hell time is it?"

"About ten to four," replied the reporter instead.

He blurted to Emily, "the clock in the interrogation room?

"Oh," she said, guiding him to the van, "it was fast." Half an hour later Michael O'Neil arrived from the motel where the bankers' party had been interrupted. He explained that everyone had got out safely, but there'd been no time to render the device safe. The explosion was quite impressive. The material was probably Semtex, judging from the

Connections 8   THE GIFT OF TIME   Paul Stuart

smell. He added more information. It was the only explosive ever to have its own FAQ on the Internet, which answered questions like: Was it named after an idyllic, pastoral village? (yes). Was it mass produced and shipped throughout the world, as the late President Vaclav Havel claimed? (no). And was Semtex the means by which its inventor committed suicide? (not exactly; yes, an employee at the plant did blow himself up intentionally, but he had not been one of the inventors).

Emily smiled as O'Neil recounted this trivia.

Steve Nichols called and told her they were on the way to deliver the other suspect, Ladislav Tolkev. He explained that since she'd broken the case, it made sense for her to process the suspects.

As they waited for Nichols to arrive O'Neil asked, "so, how did you do it? All I know is you called me about three, I guess, and told me to get choppers and a communications team ready. You hoped to have some details about the location of the attack in about forty-five minutes. But you didn't tell me what was going on."

"I didn't have much time," Emily explained. "What happened was that I found out, after wasting nearly an hour, that Kirov was kinesics-proof. So I had to trick him. I took a break at three and talked to the tech boys. It seems you can speed up analogue clocks by changing the voltage and frequency of the current in the wiring. They changed the current in that part of the building so the clock started running fast."

Connections 8   THE GIFT OF TIME   Paul Stuart

O'Neil smiled. "That was the byword for this case, remember. You said it yourself. 'Remember we have two and a half hours. We've got to move fast...'"

Emily continued, "I remembered Kirov started lecturing that media idiot about his cause. I called him and said that if he asked Kirov why he picked those particular victims, I'd give him an exclusive interview. Then I called you to set up the search teams. I went back into the interrogation room. I had to make sure Kirov didn't notice the clock was running fast, so I debated philosophy with him."

"Philosophy?"

"Well, Wikipedia philosophy. Not the real thing. You and the Crime Scene people found out that it was probably a bomb and that it was planted in a large room with a stage. When the clock in the interrogation room hit four I had Albert call me and pretend a bomb had gone off and killed people but the stage had absorbed a lot of the blast. That was just enough information to make Kirov believe it had really happened. Then all I had to do was walk him past the reporter, who asked why those particular victims. Kirov couldn't help himself from lecturing."

"It was very close."

"True. Ten minutes meant the difference between life and death for two hundred people."

An unmarked vehicle arrived and a handcuffed prisoner was pulled unceremoniously out. A large bandage covered much of his head and the side of his face. O'Neil stared at him silently.

Connections 8   THE GIFT OF TIME   Paul Stuart

"Good luck with this one, Emily. He's the toughest I've ever seen and I've seen some bad ones. Cartel drug lords and al-Qaeda terrorists are positively chatty compared with him. Not a single word. Just sits and stares at you. He's all yours."

"I'll do what I can," she replied. "There's enough forensic evidence to put them away for twenty years or so."

They said their goodbyes. Emily waited until all except O'Neil and the newly arrived prisoner had departed. Then Emily laughed and so did the prisoner.

"What's going on?" asked O'Neil.

Emily stepped forward and unlocked the handcuffs securing the wrists of her beloved Books. He removed the swaddling, revealing no injuries.

"Thank you," he said. Those two words were the first he'd uttered in over three hours. "I'll keep these handcuffs. Might come in useful at home," he said, risking a lustful look at Emily.

Emily knew what he was meaning and felt the familiar warmth begin down below, but moved on to continue her explanation.

"Ladislav Tolkev is in a lot more serious condition than I let on. He was shot in the head during the arrest and will probably be in a vegetative state for the rest of his life. Which might not be that long. I knew Nichols would want to have part of the case, but we didn't want that. I wanted the only suspect we had, so I needed to give Nichols someone."

Connections 8   THE GIFT OF TIME   Paul Stuart

"So you just deceived our own side?"

"Technically, yes, but I wasn't sure I could trust Nichols in such a situation."

"Three hours," Books was warming up now. "Three hours. You owe me, Emily."

"You'll get your reward," she promised.

"I'll hang on to these, then," he said, and pocketed the handcuffs with a glint in his eye.

O'Neil still had many questions he wanted to ask.
"What about..."

He got no further as Books shot him a glance that shook him to the core. He'd never seen eyes like those. Emily saw the silent exchange and smiled to herself.

"I guess that's it then," O'Neil concluded, shaken and keen to be as far away as possible.

"I think so," Emily said. "Oh, one more thing."

"What's that?" O'Neil asked.

"My friend here. You never saw him. As far as you're concerned he doesn't exist."

"But, I don't understand," he said.

"You don't need to. You'll find the report that you will submit to your superior on your desk by the time you arrive in the morning. Sign and date it. Then say nothing to anybody, no matter who asks."

O'Neil looked at Books, was treated to another special look, and decided to leave immediately.

Emily put her watch back on her wrist and looked at it.

"Come on then. Time we went home."

Connections 8   THE GIFT OF TIME   Paul Stuart

Books smiled at her and they walked towards her car, each planning the night's activity.

Each was also silently praying that Russian activity had been dealt with. And any follow-up discouraged. Each wondered whether there was more to come and feared that there may be. Each kept their worst fears inside, because each knew more was to come.

Connections 8   THE GIFT OF TIME   Paul Stuart

GAME: A YEAR AGO

The worst fear is the fear that follows you into your own home. Fear you lock in with you when you close and bolt the door at night. Fear that cozies up to you twenty-four hours a day, relentless and arrogant, like cancer. It insinuates itself deep into your core.

The diminutive woman, ninety-one years old, white hair tied back in jaunty style, sat at the window of her ground floor apartment, looking out over the neat road and parkland. Save for the early morning arrival and mid-afternoon departure of the schoolchildren, the day promised nothing more exciting than dog walkers and the occasional delivery van. It was a normal placid day. But she herself was not. She was agitated and took no pleasure in the view she'd enjoyed for six years.

She sipped her tea and took some small pleasure in the sliver of autumn sunlight resting on her hands and arms. The flicker of leaves outside, copper and gold. Was that all she had left? Miniscule comforts like this? And not very comforting at that.

Susan Lennox hadn't quite worked out what they were up to. But one thing was clear: taking over her life was the goal; like a flag to be captured.

Three months ago she had met the Westons at a charity coffee morning. It was for a Jewish youth organization, though neither the name nor appearance of the two suggested that was their religious or ethnic background. Still, they had

Connections 8   THE GIFT OF TIME   Paul Stuart

seemed right at home and referred to many of the leaders of the youth group as if they'd been friends for years. They'd spent a solid hour talking to Susan alone, seemingly fascinated by her life history, and explaining how they'd come there from London to 'consummate' the several business ventures John had set up for Miriam. They were building a property portfolio, and were interested in purchasing Susan's apartment. They promised, as part of the deal, that she could remain there until her passing and that the rent would be at a favourable rate. From Susan's point of view, it meant she could release the capital locked up in the property and help her family sooner rather than later. Of course, the harsh reality was that the offer made by the Weston's was nowhere near market value, and she would still have to bear the cost of management fees and other sundry items. She may be old in years, but those years had brought wisdom.

They had made their pitch over a rather good lunch, which they insisted was their treat. They were charming in an upper middle class kind of way, and were also enthusiastically curious about the apartment, the development in which it was situated and her life in particular. Their eyes widened when she told them she also had another apartment on the same development. They'd been looking for a place to stay while they explored the area and, so far, hadn't been able to find anything suitable. Susan's second apartment, known as the Garden Apartment, was on the rental market but was priced

Connections 8   THE GIFT OF TIME   Paul Stuart

high to keep out the riff raff, she'd said, laughing. She would, though, drop it to fair market value for the Westons.

Deal.

Still, Susan had learned about the world from her husband. There were formalities to be adhered to and due diligence to be done. He may have passed away, but she could hear him in her head and heart.

There was, of course, that one bit of concern. It seemed a bit odd that a fifty something mother and a son in his late twenties would be taking an apartment together, when neither seemed disabled. But life circumstances are fluid. Susan could imagine situations in which she might find herself living with a family member not a husband. Maybe Miriam's husband had just died and this was temporary, until the emotional turmoil settled.

And Susan certainly didn't know what to make of the fact that while the Garden Apartment featured three bedrooms, the new neighbours appeared to be using only one bedroom. The other two were for storage.

Odd indeed.

But Susan thought the best of people. She always had. The pair had been nice to her and, most important, treated her like an adult. It was astonishing to Susan how many people thought that once you reached seventy or eighty, let alone ninety, you were really an infant. That you couldn't order for yourself, that you didn't know who Lady Gaga was.

Connections 8   THE GIFT OF TIME   Paul Stuart

"Oh, my," she'd nearly said to one patronizing waitress. "I've forgotten how this knife works. Could you cut up my food for me?"

For the first few weeks the Westons seemed the model tenants. Respectful of landlady and premises, polite and quiet. That was important to Sarah. Also, she didn't see much of them. Not at first.

But soon their paths began to cross with more and more frequency. Susan would return from a shopping trip with her friend, Carolyn, and there would be Miriam and John on the front steps or, if the day was cool or wet, in the tiny lobby, sitting on the couch beside the letter boxes.

They brightened when they saw her and insisted she sat with them. They pelted her with stories and observations and jokes. And they could be counted on to ask questions relentlessly. What charities was she involved with? Any family members still alive? Close friends? New to the area they asked her to recommend shops, solicitors, estate agents, accountants, hinting at large reserves of cash they had to put to work soon.

John pronounced solemnly, "Property is the way to go."

"It's also a good way to get your balls handed to you son, unless you're very, very sharp." Susan had not always been a demure, retiring widow.

She began to wonder if a Nigerian scam was looming, but they never pitched to her. Maybe they were what they seemed: oddballs from London, of

Connections 8   THE GIFT OF TIME   Paul Stuart

some means, hoping for financial success and an entrée into the level of society that had never really been available to people like them.

Ultimately, Susan decided, it was their style that turned her off. The charm of the first month faded.

Miriam, also a short woman though inches taller than Sarah, wore loud, glittery clothes that clashed with her dark, leathery skin. If she didn't focus, she tended to speak over and around the conversation, ricocheting against topics that had little to do with what you believed you were speaking about. She wouldn't look you in the eye and she hovered close. Saying, "No thanks," to her was apparently synonymous with "Yes, of course."

"This place, Susan," Miriam would say, shaking her head gravely. "Doesn't it tire you out?

John often wore a shabby sardonic grin, as if he'd caught somebody trying to cheat him. He was fleshy big, but strong, too. You could imagine his grainy picture in a newspaper above a story in which the word 'snapped' appeared in a quote from the local police.

If he wasn't grumbling or snide, he'd be snorting as he told jokes, which were never very funny and usually bordered on the off-colour.

But avoiding them was petrol on a flame. When they sensed she was avoiding them they redoubled their efforts to graze their way into her life, coming to her front door at any hour, offering presents and advice and always the questions about

Connections 8   THE GIFT OF TIME   Paul Stuart

her. John would appear to take care of the small handyman tasks around Susan's apartment. Carolyn's husband, Daniel, was the building's part time maintenance man, but John befriended him and took over on some projects to give Daniel a few hours off here and there.

Susan believed the Westons actually waited, hiding behind their own door, listening for sounds of footsteps padding, and Susan was a very quiet padder. Still the Westons would spring out, tall son and short mother, joining her as if this were a rendezvous planned for weeks.

If they steamed up to her on the outside, they attached themselves like leeches and no amount of "Better be going" or "have a good day," could dislodge them. She stopped inviting them into her apartment, but when they tracked her down outside they would simply walk in with her when she returned.

Miriam would take her groceries and put them away and John would sit forward on the couch with a glass of water his mother brought him and grin in that got-you way of his. Miriam sat down with tea or coffee for the ladies and inquired how Susan was feeling; did she ever go away? was she careful about things?

Oh, Lord, leave me alone.

Susan spoke to the solicitor and property management agent and learned there was nothing she could do to evict them. And it got worse. They'd accidently let slip facts about Susan's life that they

Connections 8   THE GIFT OF TIME   Paul Stuart

shouldn't have known. Bank accounts she had, meetings she'd been to with wealthy bankers. They'd been spying. She wondered if they'd been going through her post, which would be illegal. But she doubted the police would be very interested.

And then, a month ago, irritation became fear.

Typically, they'd poured inside after her as she returned from shopping alone. Miriam had scooped the bags from her hand and John had, out of courtesy, taken her key and opened the door.

Susan had been too flustered to protest, which would have done little good anyway, she now knew.

They'd sat for fifteen minutes, water and tea at hand, talking about who knew what, best of friends, and then Miriam had picked up her large purse and gone to use the toilet and headed for Susan's bedroom.

Susan stood, saying she'd prefer the woman to use the guest bathroom, but John had turned his knotted brows her way and barked, "Sit down! Mother can pick whichever she wants."

And Susan had, half thinking she was about to be beaten to death. But the son slipped back to conversation mode and rambled on about yet another property deal he was thinking of doing.

Susan, shaken, merely nodded and tried to sip her tea. She knew the woman was riffling through her personal things. Or planting a camera or listening device.

Or worse.

Connections 8   THE GIFT OF TIME   Paul Stuart

When Miriam returned, fifteen minutes later, she glanced at her son and he rose. In eerie unison they marched out of the apartment.

Susan searched but she couldn't find any eavesdropping devices and couldn't tell if anything was disturbed or missing; and that might have been disastrous as she had close to three quarters of a million pounds in cash and jewels tucked away in her bedroom.

But they'd been up to no good and she was frightened. She was also angered by their lack of manners. They had infected what time she had left on this earth and were destroying it. Time she wanted to spend simply and harmlessly, visiting those she cared for, directing her money where it would do most good, volunteering for charities, working on the needlepoints she loved so much, a passion that was a legacy from her mother.

And yet those pleasures were being denied her.

Susan Lennox was a woman of mettle, serene though she seemed and diminutive though she was. She had a steely spirit but the physical package to give it play was gone. She was ninety-one, as tiny and frail as a leaf in the garden. And her mind, too. She wasn't as quick and her memory was not what it had been. What could she do about the pair that she thought of as the "Beasts"?

Now, sitting in the parlour, she dropped her hands to her knees. Nothing occurred to her. It seemed hopeless.

Connections 8   THE GIFT OF TIME   Paul Stuart

Then, a key clattered in the lock. Susan's breath sucked in. She assumed that somehow the Beasts had copied her key and she expected to see them now.

But, no. She sighed in relief to see Carolyn return from shopping.

Were tears in her eyes?

"What's the matter?" Susan asked.

"Nothing," the woman responded quickly.

Too quickly.

"Yes, yes, yes. But if something were the matter, give me a clue, dear."

The solid housekeeper carried the groceries into the kitchen, making sure she didn't look at Sarah.

Yes, crying.

"There's nothing wrong, Sarah. Really."

She returned to the living room and instinctively, the woman straightened a lace doily.

"Was it him? What did he do?"

Susan knew he was involved somehow. Both Miriam and John disliked Carolyn, as did most of Susan's friends, but John seemed contemptuous of the woman, as if she mounted a campaign to limit access to Susan. Which she did. In fact, several times she had actually stepped in front of John to prevent him from following Susan into her apartment. Susan had thought he'd been about to hit the poor woman.

"Please, it's nothing."

Connections 8   THE GIFT OF TIME   Paul Stuart

Carolyn was five feet six inches tall and probably weighed 180 pounds. Yet the elderly woman now rose and looked up at her.

"Carolyn. Tell me." The voice left no room for debate.

"I got home from shopping? I was outside?

Statements as questions. The telltale sign of uncertainty.

"I came back from the shop and was talking to him and then he came up and, just out of nowhere, he asks whether I'd heard about the burglary.

"Where?"

"Around here somewhere. I said I hadn't. He said somebody broke in and stole this woman's papers. Like banking papers and wills and deeds and shares. He said she got robbed and these men took all her things. He said he was worried about you."

"Me?"

"Yes, Susan. And he didn't want to make you upset but he was worried and did I know where you kept things like that? Was there a safe somewhere? He said he wanted to make sure they were protected."

The woman wiped her face. Susan had thought her name was Carolyn at first, as one would think, given her pedigree and appearance. But no, her mother and father had named her after the town in America, where they dreamed of visiting one day.

Susan found a tissue and handed it to the woman. This was certainly alarming. It seemed to

Connections 8   THE GIFT OF TIME   Paul Stuart

represent a new level of invasiveness. Still, John Weston's probing was constant and familiar, like a low-grade fever, which Carolyn had her own mettle to withstand.

No, something else had happened.

"And?"

"No, really. Just that."

Susan herself could be persistent, too. "Come now...."

"He...I think it was maybe a coincidence. Didn't mean anything."

Nothing the Westons did was a coincidence.

"Tell me, anyway," Susan said.

"Then he said," the woman offered, choking back a sob, "if I didn't tell him, he wouldn't be able to protect you. And if those papers were stolen, you'd lose all your money. And then he said my daughter might have to leave her school."

"He said that?" Susan asked.

Carolyn was crying now. "How would he know I paid for your daughter's private school? Why would he find that out?"

Because he and his mother did their homework. They asked their questions, like chickens pecking up seed and stones.

"I got mad and said I couldn't wait until their rental is over and he and his mother went away forever. And he said they weren't going anywhere. He said they can stay forever as long as they pay the rent and don't break the terms of the lease. Is that true, Sarah?"

Connections 8   THE GIFT OF TIME   Paul Stuart

"Yes, Carolyn, it is true."

She rose and sat down at the Steinway piano she'd owned for nearly twenty years. It had been a present from her husband. She played a few bars of Chopin, her favourite composer.

Carolyn continued. "When he left he said to say hello to Daniel and say hi to Rosa. He said she's a pretty girl. Pretty like her mother."

Carolyn was shivering now, tears were flowing. Susan turned from the piano and touched her friend on the shoulder. "It's all right, dear. You did the right thing to tell me."

The tears slowed and finally stopped. A tissue made its way around her face.

After a long silence, Susan said, "When Mark and I were in Malaysia we went to this preserve."

"Like a nature preserve?"

"That's right. And there was this moth he showed us. It's called an Atlas moth. Now, it's very big. Its wingspan is six or eight inches across."

"That's big," agreed Carolyn.

"But they're still moths. The guide pointed at it. 'How can it defend itself? What does it have? Teeth? No. Venom? No. Claws? No.' But then the guide pointed out the markings on this moth's wings. And it looked just like a snake's head! It was exactly like a cobra. Same colour, everything."

"Really, Susan?"

"Really. So that predators aren't sure whether it would be safe to eat the moth or not. So they

Connections 8   THE GIFT OF TIME   Paul Stuart

usually move on to something else and leave the moth alone."

Carolyn was nodding, not at all sure where this was going.

"I'm going to do that with the Westons."

"How? Asked Carolyn.

"I'll show them the snake's head. I'm going to make them think it's too dangerous to stay here and they should move out."

"Good! How are you going to do that?"

"Did I show you my birthday present?"

"The flowers?"

"No, this."

Susan took an iPhone from her bag. She fiddled with the functions, many of which she had to figure out.

"I have a contact. Her name's Emily. She said she'd help me. She gave me this and told me to record whatever was said. When I've done that I have to send it to her. She said she will make sure these people are dealt with."

"You're going to record them, doing that? Threatening you?"

"Exactly. I was going to e-mail a copy to my solicitor, but Emily said not to worry. She said something about sending her boyfriend Books to have a word with them. She said she promised that would be enough. I hope she's right."

"But it might not be safe, Susan."

"I'm sure it won't be. But it doesn't look like I have much choice, have I?"

Connections 8   THE GIFT OF TIME   Paul Stuart

Then Susan noticed that Carolyn was frowning, looking away.

The older woman said, "I know what you're thinking. They'll just go and find somebody else to torture and do the same thing to them"

"Yes, that's what I was thinking."

Susan said softly, "but in the jungle, you know, it's not the moth's job to protect the whole world. It's the moth's job to stay alive. Emily told me not to worry. Books will make sure they don't worry anybody ever again. He sounds scary."

Connections 8   THE GIFT OF TIME   Paul Stuart

GAME: PRESENT DAY

"You'd like me to find somebody?" the man asked the solemn woman sitting across from him. "Missing person?"

The woman corrected him solemnly, "Body. Not somebody. A body."

"Excuse me?"

"A body. I want to know where a body is. Where it's buried."

"Oh."

Books remained thoughtfully attentive, but now that he thought the woman might be a crackpot he wanted mostly to leave. But he had been asked to meet the woman and, as the request had come from his beloved Emily, it was not merely a request. Also, he knew that it had come from a higher source. Her father, Frank. That meant it was a secret operation that involved national security and could not be ignored. The woman believed he was a private investigator whom she could hire and could therefore expect payment by results. The cover afforded Books some latitude in how he dealt with the matter. He kept his attention on the substantial woman across his desk, which was bisected by a slash of summer light reflected off a nearby block of flats across the road.

Connections 8 THE GIFT OF TIME Paul Stuart

"Okay. Keep going," Books said. He already knew her name, but wanted her to tell him as a way of making her feel more comfortable. Old tricks are the best.

"Carolyn. Call me Carolyn," she said.

"A body, you were saying Carolyn."

"A murdered woman. A friend."

Books leaned forward, showing interest. He already knew the facts as far as the team knew them, but it wouldn't hurt to let her give her version. You never know when something new or contradictory was going to pop out of the woodwork.

He had one word in his head: 'Game.' It was hard to define, and he'd not talked about it with anyone except Emily. It was his own concept, and it meant all the interesting, the weird and the captivating. Game was that indefinable aspect of love and work and everything else, including sport, that kept you engaged, that got the juices flowing, that kept you off balance.

People had Game or they didn't. If not, break up. Jobs had Game, or they didn't. And if not, quit. Another thing about Game. You couldn't fake it.

Books had a feeling this woman, and this case, had Game.

"A year ago, I lost someone I was close to," she said.

Connections 8   THE GIFT OF TIME   Paul Stuart

"I'm sorry," He offered.

"Here." Carolyn opened a large bag and took out what must have been fifty sheets of paper, rumpled, grey, torn. Actual newspaper clippings too, which you didn't see much, as opposed to computer printouts, though there were some of those, too. She set them on his desk, and re-arranged them carefully. Pushed the stack forward.

"What's this?" he asked.

"Newspaper stories about her, Susan Lennox. She was the one murdered."

Something familiar, Books believed. London is a surprisingly small town when it comes to crime. News of horrific violence spreads fast, like a dot of oil on water, and the hard details seat themselves deep in public memory.

Books scanned the material quickly. The story confirmed the briefing he had been given earlier. Susan Lennox was an elderly woman killed by a bizarre couple. There was another name in the stories, one of the witnesses, and she was sitting in front of him. Carolyn had been Susan's friend and her husband was the part-time maintenance man.

"You realise that I don't work for nothing. There will be a fee," He said.

"Of course. I expected as much. Emily helped Susan when the odd couple were bothering her. She

Connections 8 THE GIFT OF TIME Paul Stuart

said her friend Books would sort it all out. I never met him, but he sounded scary enough. I thought he'd been successful and warned them off, but now she's dead and I don't know what to think or do." Carolyn was near to tears.

"I'll tell you what I'll do. As my friend Emily kindly recommended me, I won't charge for this first session."

Books smiled his winning smile and they agreed a fee per day, or by outcome, whichever was the sooner. He needed her to believe he was a private investigator, rather than anything else.

"Okay," she said. "But I don't know your name. What do I call you?"

"You may call me Ray. Ray Reader."

Books smiled at his own cleverness and because this matter had Game written all over it.

They had set Books up in a scuffed, boring, nondescript office in a building those same adjectives apply to. The building featured dentists, accountants, one-man law firms, a plastic surgeon and himself. He often thought that there wasn't much left in life for people to deal with. They could get teeth and boobs fixed, taxes paid and legal problems sorted out. His office was not used apart from the occasions when the team needed such a front for their activities. It had been deliberately

Connections 8   THE GIFT OF TIME   Paul Stuart

labelled as a Private Investigation firm because that allowed almost anything to be done without attracting unwanted attention.

Books finished reading the account of the murder. To be accurate, he skimmed it and pushed the material back to Carolyn. Definitely Game, he thought.

The story was interesting, as Carolyn had suggested it would be. Susan's itinerant younger days, a bit of a rebel, irreverent and clever. He decided he might have liked the woman. He was already upset that the Westons had beaten her to death with a hammer, wrapped the body in a waste bag, and dumped her in an unmarked grave. They saw her as a wealthy, elderly vulnerable woman with no family, living alone. A perfect target. They rented the apartment on the ground floor and began a relentless campaign to take control of her life. She had finally had enough of them and, helped by Emily, she had tried to record them threatening her. They'd caught her in the act, though, and forced her to sign a contract selling them the building for next to nothing. They immobilized her with a Taser and bludgeoned her to death.

That afternoon Carolyn returned from shopping and found her missing. Knowing that the Westons had been asking about her valuables and

Connections 8   THE GIFT OF TIME   Paul Stuart

that Susan was going to record them threatening her, she suspected what had happened. She called the police. Given that, and the fact that a routine search revealed the Westons had criminal history, officers responded immediately. They found some fresh blood in the garage. That was enough for a search warrant. The Taser was found, with Susan's skin in the barbs, a hammer with John's prints and Susan's blood and hair, and duct tape with both Susan's and Miriam's DNA. A roll of rubbish bags, too, three of them missing.

Computer forensics experts found the couple had tried to hack into Susan's financial affairs, without success. Also found were insurance documents covering close to seven hundred thousand pounds in cash and jewellery kept on the premises. Two necklaces identified as Susan's were found in Miriam's jewellery box. All of the valuables had been stolen.

The defence claimed that drug gangs had broken in and killed her. Or, as an alternative, that Susan had gone senile and wandered off by herself on a bus or train.

Juries hate lame excuses and it took the Weston panel all of four hours to convict. The pair were sentenced to life imprisonment. The farewell in

Connections 8   THE GIFT OF TIME   Paul Stuart

the courtroom with mother and son embracing like spouses, made for a really nauseating picture.

"I kept hoping the police would find her remains," Carolyn said.

John's car had been spotted several days before Susan disappeared in Hertfordshire, where he was reportedly looking at property to add to his portfolio. It was assumed the body had been dumped there.

Carolyn continued, "I don't know about her religion, the Jewish one, but I'm sure it's important to be buried and have a gravestone and have people say some words over you. To have people come and see you. Don't you think, Mr. Reader?"

He didn't have a view one way or another, but he now nodded.

"The problem is, you see, this is a simple death."

"Simple?" the woman sat forward, brows furrowing a bit.

"Not to make little of it, understand me," Books added quickly, seeing the dismay on her face. "It's just that it's open and shut, you know? Nasty criminals, good evidence. No love children, no hidden treasure that was never recorded, no conspiracy theories. Fast conviction. With a simple death, people lose interest. The leads go cold very

Connections 8   THE GIFT OF TIME   Paul Stuart

rapidly. I'm saying it could be expensive for me to take on the case."

"I can pay you three thousand pounds. No more than that."

"That would buy you about twenty-five hours of my time. I'll forget the expenses. Have you thought this through?"

Books thought it was time to appear business like.

"What do you mean?" she asked.

"Well, it's a terrible crime but justice has been done. If I start searching, I may have to ask you things. You'll have to relive the incident. And, well, sometimes when people look into the past, they find things they wish they hadn't."

"What could that be?"

"Maybe there'd be no way to recover the body, even if I find it. Maybe it was, let's say, disrespected when it was disposed of."

Carolyn had not considered this, he could tell. People rarely do. But she said, "I want to say a prayer at her grave, wherever it is. I don't care about anything else."

Books pulled a blank contract form from his desk drawer. They both signed it. Also, on a whim, he penned in a discounted hourly rate. He'd noticed pictures of her three children when she'd opened her

Connections 8   THE GIFT OF TIME   Paul Stuart

handbag to find her driving licence for the agreement. They were teenagers and the parents were surely facing the horror of student expenses.

"All right," he said to her. "Let me keep these and I'll get to work. Give me your home and mobile numbers."

A hesitation. "E-mail please. Only e-mail." She wrote it down.

"No problem. No phone call?" He asked.

"No, please don't. See, I mentioned to my husband I was thinking about doing this and he said it wasn't a good idea."

"Why?"

She nodded at the news clippings. "It's in there somewhere. There was a man working for the Westons, the police think. Daniel's worried he'd find out if we started looking for the body. He's probably dangerous."

Glad you mentioned it, Books thought wryly. "Okay. E-mail it is." He rose.

Carolyn stepped forward and actually hugged him, tears in her eyes. She took her time composing herself and left.

Books pulled the stack of clippings closer, to make more notes, and to read, in particular, about the Weston's possible accomplice. He wondered if he would be in danger. It didn't worry him at all. Game

Connections 8   THE GIFT OF TIME   Paul Stuart

had to come with a little risk, otherwise it wasn't Game.

But none of this explained Emily's real reason for her involvement or that of their elite team.

Connections 8   THE GIFT OF TIME   Paul Stuart

-2-

"Thank you for coming," Books said. "My name is Reader. Ray Reader. Please take a seat."

Assistant Commissioner Andrew Cushing was not a happy man but he eventually and slowly sat down facing the desk and the man behind it. He chose not to hide his anger.

"I had no choice. As you are well aware. I was more or less kidnapped, thrown into a car and frog marched here. How dare you treat me in this way? Do you know who I am? You are treading on very thin ice, I can tell you."

Books rested his hands on his desk, fingers interlocking. He was completely relaxed and not a little amused.

"I should apologise," he began," but I won't. Let me explain. There is currently some research into the death and disappearance of a woman called Susan Lennox. Your force carried out the initial investigation and two people were convicted and imprisoned for life. I see you've brought the file with you. Most helpful." Books stopped.

"Again, I had no choice. It was already in the car waiting for me. I've been used as nothing more than a courier!" Cushing's cheeks, already purple, took on a much more unfortunate hue, which indicated heart problems.

Connections 8   THE GIFT OF TIME   Paul Stuart

"Please, calm down, Mr. Cushing."

"Assistant Commissioner!"

"If you'll allow me, I'll explain, Mr. Cushing."

Books was deliberately baiting his man.

"The investigation by your force has been found to be unreliable. It didn't uncover certain aspects of the lives of the main protagonists. Not thorough, at all. I have been tasked to revisit the case and close the loopholes. It has been taken out of your hands. The file will remain with me. You will forget you've ever been here or that we have met." Books paused, assessing reaction.

"I beg your pardon! What the hell is going on here?" Puce had taken over his cheeks and he literally shook with anger.

"Please, Mr. Cushing, calm down. You'll harm yourself. It is a matter of national security and that's all I am able to tell you. I understand your point of view, I really do, but, if you'll take my advice, you'll have a glass of water, compose yourself, help me today and then walk away while you still have your uniform and rank. I have no axe to grind as far as you are concerned."

Books was moving into business mode and was impatient to have the man removed from his office with as little fuss as possible. He treated the

Connections 8   THE GIFT OF TIME   Paul Stuart

senior policeman to a look that shook the man to the core. There was no wriggle room available.

"Now, Mr. Cushing," Books maintained the form of address to show who was in charge and he was also enjoying his discomfort. "Please tell me what you know about the case."

"Those two were very odd. I mean, Mother and son, with only one bed in the place. Makes my skin crawl. Think about it." The policeman stopped.

"I'd rather not," admitted Books.

Cushing continued, "So you need to know where they dumped the body?"

"Yes. Or, more accurately, her friend Carolyn wants to know. She's religious, you know."

"I looked through the file in the car on the way here. Didn't have much time."

"Don't bother with that. Excuses won't wash. It was your force, your responsibility."

"In my opinion, the best bet for a corpse is somewhere like Camber Sands, because of the quicksand." Cushing looked at Books.

"But people rarely get completely sucked under. It's usually the tide that gets them because they're stuck. The body would be easily found." Books dismissed Cushing's offering. "But it's worth looking at, I suppose."

Connections 8   THE GIFT OF TIME   Paul Stuart

"It certainly is. Particularly as CCTV has their car in that area and the locals were told the Westons were checking out property to buy." Cushing said.

Books flicked open the file and came across a sub-file which was labelled John Weston. Many of the documents were his own notes and records, and a lot of them had to do with property. Construction paperwork, crane permits, street access permissions, details of foundations, maps, sketches, drawings. All were multi-million pound projects that John couldn't possibility have been involved with unless he had Susan Lennox's money.

"When was Weston at Camber Sands?"

"A couple of days before she disappeared."

"Before? Was there any record of him being there after she disappeared?"

"No. That's where the grassy knoll effect comes in. Dallas. Kennedy's assassination. The other gunman."

"I don't believe there was one. It was Oswald. Alone."

"I'm not arguing that. My point is that the Westons probably did have an accomplice. He's the one who got rid of the body. In his car. So there were no records of Weston returning."

"Why would he be the one who dumped the body, though?" Books asked.

Connections 8   THE GIFT OF TIME   Paul Stuart

Cushing tapped the file. "Just after they killed her, the Westons were seen in public so they'd have an alibi. They would have hired somebody to dump the body. Probably somebody connected." He smiled inwardly at his use of the transatlantic vernacular.

"You mean to organized crime?" Books asked, not hiding his sarcasm.

"We think it was some low level figure. The Westons had connections with crime in Nottingham, Glasgow and Manchester. Maybe other places too. They must have found some 'friend' here. They would have paid him from Mrs. Lennox's stolen cash and jewellery."

Books noted that Assistant Commissioner Cushing had called her Mrs. Lennox. That was good. It showed he was calming down and beginning to be helpful. Books hoped the man had realised he had no other option, if he wanted to save his dignity and, more importantly, his retirement pension. For retire he would, even though he didn't yet know it.

"Any leads to him?" Books asked.

"No, but he was after the fact and nobody really gave a monkey's. They had their suspects, so why waste resources?"

"The couple...." Books began his next question.

Connections 8   THE GIFT OF TIME   Paul Stuart

"They're mother and son, I wouldn't call them a couple."

"The couple," Books ignored the needless and tiresome interruption. "Did they say anything about the third man?"

Cushing looked at Books as if he'd taken leave of his senses. "It was a gang related murder, unless she decided to take herself off on a cruise and forgot to tell anybody. To quote the couple, there was no third man."

Books gave him a withering look and shook his head slowly. "Your car is waiting, Mr. Cushing. Go home. You won't be required at work anymore. Your belongings will be delivered to you. Please don't try to fight this or things will not go well for you. Your pension will be paid every month, unless you poke your head above my parapet at any time. Enjoy the rest. Go fishing, watch the TV, take a holiday. Whatever you want, but do not get involved in anything to do with police work, and that includes any contact with colleagues. I'd like to say you've earned it, but....."

Books was finished. He lowered his head as if to study the file. It was over. Assistant Commissioner Andrew Cushing was dismissed. He felt his right arm being gently, but firmly, gripped from behind as he rose from his chair. He was

Connections 8   THE GIFT OF TIME   Paul Stuart

guided out of the office and out into the big wide world of retirement and all its accompanying uncertainties.

Connections 8   THE GIFT OF TIME   Paul Stuart

USE TIME WISELY

-1-

Hat in hand. There was no other way to describe it. Aside from the flashy secretary, the middle-aged man in jeans and a sports coat was alone, surveying the glassy waiting room. He checked out the flowers, which he noted were fresh, the art, which he recognized as originals and the secretary herself, whom he saw as decorative.

How many waiting rooms had he been in just like this, over his thirty odd years in the industry? Mike O'Connor wondered. He couldn't even begin to guess. He examined a purple orchid, trying to shake the thought as he realised he was actually there begging, hat in hand.

But he couldn't. Nor could he ditch the consequent thought that this was his last chance.

There was a faint buzz from somewhere on the woman's desk. She was blonde, and O'Connor, who tended to judge women by comparing them to his wife to whom he had awarded a very high standard, thought she was attractive enough. Attractive enough for what he couldn't say, but she wouldn't make the grade in terms of leading roles. Perhaps a pretty walk-on. Maybe. At a push.

She put the phone down.

Connections 8   THE GIFT OF TIME   Paul Stuart

"He'll see you now, Mr. O'Connor," she purred as she rose from her seat to get the door for him.

"That's okay, I'll get it. Good luck," he added. He'd seen her reading a script.

She didn't know what he meant.

He closed the door behind him and Andrew Feltham, a fit man in his early thirties, wearing expensive trousers and a dark grey shirt with no tie, rose to greet him.

"Mike. My God, it's been two years."

"Your father's funeral."

"That's right."

"How's your Mother doing?"

"Scandal! She's seeing somebody. He's only five years younger than her and wears an earring!"

"Give her my best, will you?"

"Of course."

Feltham's father had been a director of photography for a while on O'Connor's TV show in the eighties. He was a talented man, wily, a voice of reason in the chaotic world of weekly television.

They carried on a bit of conversation about their own families. Neither were particularly interested, but such was the protocol of business throughout the world.

Connections 8   THE GIFT OF TIME   Paul Stuart

Then, because this wasn't just business, the moment arrived. Feltham tapped the packet of material that O'Connor had sent.

"I read it, Mike. It's an interesting concept. Tell me a little more."

O'Connor knew the difference between 'it's interesting' and 'I'm interested." He swallowed and began to describe the proposal for a new TV series in more depth.

Michael O'Connor had been hot in the late seventies and eighties. He'd starred in several peak time dramas, the most successful of which was about a Metropolitan Murder Squad, formed specifically to tackle the frightening rise in knife and gun crime in London. With the benefit of hindsight, it now seemed way ahead of its time and uncannily prophetic. It was considered cutting edge television and used techniques, such as hand held cameras, which made for gritty and sometimes uncomfortable watching. The writers, including O'Connor himself, weren't afraid to blow away a main character occasionally or let the villain get off. A service Met. police officer, who was a good friend of O'Connor's, was the consultant for the show and he insisted that the details were accurate. It dealt with religion, abortion, race, terrorism, sex, violent crime, anything in fact. However, as is the way of things,

Connections 8   THE GIFT OF TIME   Paul Stuart

it's time was up and it was taken off air, wheeled out occasionally on minority stations showing drama from an earlier age.

O'Connor couldn't get work. At least not the kind of work that was inspired and challenging. He sent agents with absurd premises or hackneyed, inferior versions of his own show, or sitcoms for which he had neither patience nor talent. His income consisted of gradually diminishing payments from when his creations were aired, which was not often these days. It all went to help pay for his daughter's university expenses, in an effort to keep her student debt to a reasonable level.

O'Connor was interested in more than acting. He had a vision. Unfortunately, it seemed that producers wanted something that was completely original and yet had been wildly successful in the past. There is some truth to that irony. For years he had it in mind to do a project that was fresh but still rooted in TV history. Each week would have a different story, sometimes drama, sometimes comedy, sometimes science fiction. In fact, all genres under the same umbrella.

He'd written a proposal and the pilot script and then hawked it to every organization and channel he could think of. Not one of them had shown any degree of interest. Now, Andrew Feltham

Connections 8   THE GIFT OF TIME   Paul Stuart

was his last chance. He had avoided going to him until then because he didn't want to pressure him unfairly by using the man's father and his friendship. He knew, however, that Feltham himself wasn't exactly a rising star. His production companies had backed some losing TV and film project recently and he couldn't afford to take any risks.

O'Connor was, however, desperate and that was the reason he was there, hat in hand. Feltham nodded, listening attentively as O'Connor pitched his idea. He was good. He had, after all, done it many times recently. He was praying the outcome would be different this time.

There was a knock and a large man, dressed similarly to Feltham, walked into the office without being formally admitted. His youth and the reverential look he gave to Feltham told O'Connor immediately he was a production assistant, a position which was usually the backbone of most TV and film companies. The man, with an effeminate manner, treated O'Connor to an overly long smile, which was enough of a gaze to make the latter want to let him know he was straight, but thank you for the compliment.

The PA said to Feltham, "He turned it down."

"He what?"

Connections 8   THE GIFT OF TIME   Paul Stuart

"Yes. I was beside myself."

"He said he was in."

"He's not in. He's out."

The elliptical conversation, probably about an actor who'd agreed to do something but had backed out at the last minute having had a better offer, continued for a few minutes more.

As they dealt with the emergency, O'Connor tuned out and glanced at the walls of the man's office. Like many producers it was covered with posters of the shows he'd created and recent films. There were also, he noticed, some that were of films O'Connor remembered fondly from his childhood. The great classics like *The Guns of Navarone, The Dirty Dozen, The Magnificent Seven* and *Bullit*.

The actor remembered that he and Feltham's father would sometimes hang out for a beer after the week's shooting for the *Murder Squad* had finished for the day. Of course, they'd gossip about the shenanigans on the set, but they'd also talk about their shared passion: feature films. O'Connor recalled that often young Andrew would join them, their conversations helping to plant the seeds of the boy's future career.

Feltham and the bodybuilder of a production assistant concluded their discussion of the actor crisis. The producer shook his head.

Connections 8   THE GIFT OF TIME   Paul Stuart

"OK. Find somebody else, but I'm talking one day, tops."

"No problem."

Feltham grimaced. "When people make a commitment, you'd think they'd stick to it. Was it different back then?"

"Back then?"

"The *Murder Squad* days?"

"Not really. There were good people and bad people."

Feltham sighed and summarized. "To hell with the bad ones. Anyway, sorry for the interruption."

O'Connor nodded.

The producer rocked back in a sumptuous leather chair. "I've got to be honest with you, Mike."

Ah, one of the more often used rejections. O'Connor at least gave him credit for meeting with him in person to deliver the bad news. Feltham had a host of assistants who could have been detailed to deliver the message. He could even have simply posted back the material. O'Connor had, after all, been prescient enough to include a stamped, self-addressed envelope.

"We couldn't sell episodic TV like this nowadays. We have to go with what's hot. People want reality, sitcoms, traditional drama." Feltham tapped O'Connor's paperwork proposal. "This is

Connections 8   THE GIFT OF TIME   Paul Stuart

groundbreaking. But to the industry now, that word scares them. It's like it's literal; an earthquake. Natural disaster. Everybody wants formula. Syndicators want formula, stations want formula, the audience too. They want a familiar team, predictable conflicts. It's the way of the world, Mike. I wish I could help you out. My father, rest his soul, loved working on your show. He said you were a genius. But we've got to go with the trends."

"Trends change," O'Connor ventured. "Wouldn't you like to be part of a new one. Perhaps even leading one?"

"Not really." Feltham laughed. "And you know why? Because I'm a coward. We're all cowards, Mike."

O'Connor looked the man over, appraising him, digging deeper.

"There's something else, isn't there?"

Feltham placed his hands on his massive glass desk.

"What can I say? Come on, Mike, you're not a child anymore."

"This is no industry for old men," he'd say, paraphrasing W. B. Yeats' line from 'Sailing to Byzantium.'

Connections 8   THE GIFT OF TIME   Paul Stuart

In general men have a longer shelf life than women in TV and films, but there are limits. Mike O'Connor was fifty-eight years old.

"Exactly."

"I don't want to star. I might play a character from time to time, just for the fun of it. We'll have a new lead every week. We can get whoever we want."

"Oh, you can?" Feltham responded wryly to the claim.

"Or we could have a youngster of the month. Up and coming talent."

"It's brilliant, Mike. It's just not saleable."

"Well, Aaron, I've taken up enough of your time. Thanks for seeing me. I mean that. A lot of people wouldn't have."

They chatted a bit more about family and other things and then O'Connor could see it was time to go. Something in Feltham's body language said he had another meeting to take. They shook hands. O'Connor respected the fact that Feltham didn't end the conversation with 'let's get together sometime.'

O'Connor was at the door when he heard Feltham say, "Hey Mike. Hold on a minute."

The actor turned and noted the producer was looking at him closely with furrowed brows, contemplating O'Connor's flop of greying blond hair,

Connections 8 THE GIFT OF TIME Paul Stuart

the broad shoulders, trim hips. Like most professional actors Mike O'Connor stayed in shape.

"Something just occurred to me. Take a seat." Feltham nodded at the still warm chair.

O'Connor sat and looked at Feltham with an expression which betrayed his confusion. The latter had a curious smile on his face and his eyes were sparkling.

"I've got an idea."

"Which is?"

"You may not like it at first. But there's method in my madness."

"Well, sanity hasn't worked. I'll listen to madness."

"Do you play poker?"

"I can play, but haven't for ages. I once lost too much money and vowed not to repeat the mistake."

Connections 8   THE GIFT OF TIME   Paul Stuart

-2-

O'Connor and Diane were sitting on the patio of their house. It was pleasant, if modest. He sipped the wine he'd brought them both out from the kitchen.

"Thanks, lover," she said. Diane, petite, and wiry, was a real estate broker and she and O'Connor had been together for thirty years, with never an affair between them. It was a testament to the fact that not all marriages in their field of activity are doomed to fail.

She poured more wine.

The patio overlooked a pleasant valley which was tinted blue at dusk. Directly beneath them was a gorgeous house. Occasionally film crews would disappear inside, the shades would be drawn, the crew would emerge five hours later, and yet another pornographic film would soon be on the market.

"Feltham's proposing real time celebrity poker. For real money."

"Sounds sleazy," Diane said.

"I was dubious at first, too. But listen to this. It's apparently a big deal"

"Really?"

"And it's live."

"Live TV?"

"Yes."

Connections 8   THE GIFT OF TIME   Paul Stuart

"So it's live, sleazy reality TV. What makes it different?"

"Have some more wine," was O'Connor's answer.

"Uh-oh."

O'Connor explained that what set this new show, *Go For Broke,* apart from other typical celebrity poker shows was that on this one the contestants would be playing with their own money. Real money. Not for charity contributions.

"Andrew's view is that reality TV isn't real at all. Nobody's got anything to lose, there's really no risk. The people who climb walls or walk on beams are tethered, and they've got spotters everywhere. And eating worms isn't going to kill you."

She had spotted it quickly. "Get back to the part about 'our own money.'"

"The stakes are a quarter of a million. We come in with that. Then we play with cash on the table. No chips. It's all actually real."

"Are the networks behind it?" she asked.

"Oh yes. It's huge."

"Okay, it's big. We can probably get our hands on the money, but we can't afford for you to lose it. Even if you win and you make a million, it's still very risky."

Connections 8   THE GIFT OF TIME   Paul Stuart

"Oh, it's not about the money. It has nothing to do with money," Mike was trying to sound convincing.

"Then what's it about?"

"The bump."

"The bump? What is that? It sounds like a euphemism for something medical and nasty."

"Why use a dozen words when one will do?" Mike replied, before explaining to Diane exactly what Feltham had told him earlier. "A bump is a leg-up. A helping hand on your way up the greasy pole to the top. It gets your name out there where it needs to be. It doesn't guarantee you success, but it gets you in the front door, so to speak."

Diane remained silent, digesting the information, working out whether it was to her liking or not.

Mike continued, "All the contestants are like me. At a certain level, but not where they want to be. They're from a cross-section of entertainment industries, music, acting, stand-up comedy."

Diane was shaking her head and rising, much to his disappointment. Without a word she walked into the kitchen. He loved her and, more importantly, he trusted her and her judgement. Nevertheless, he couldn't help showing his disappointment.

Connections 8   THE GIFT OF TIME   Paul Stuart

She returned a moment later with a new bottle of chardonnay.

"You don't want me to do it, do you?" he asked.

"I'll answer that with one question," she replied.

He speculated: where would they get the money? Would they have to use their retirement funds? But it turned out that she was curious about something else.

"Does a full house beat a flush," she asked.

"Um, well..." he frowned.

Diane withdrew from her pocket something she'd apparently collected when she'd gone into the kitchen for the wine: a deck of cards.

"I can see you need some practice, my love," she said and snapped open the clear wrapping.

Connections 8   THE GIFT OF TIME   Paul Stuart

-3-

The bar was in Soho, on one of those streets where you can see celebs and people who want to be celebs, and people who, whether they are celebs or not, are just absolutely beautiful, or think they are.

Sammy Ralston was checking some of them out now – the women at least- and looking for starlets. He watched a lot of TV. He watched now in his small apartment, and he'd watched a lot when he was 'inside' as well, although the Islamic inmates dictated what you saw, which during the day was mostly unintelligible and, more to the point, uncomfortable as well.

He looked up and saw Jake walk through the door, shaved head, inked forearms. Huge. A biker. He wore a leather jacket with 'OAKLAND' on the back. Say no more. He stood above Ralston. Way above. "Why'd you get a table?"

"I don't know. I just did."

"Because you wanted some faggot chicken wings, or what?"

"I don't know. I just did." The repetition was edgy. Ralston was small but he didn't put up with much shit.

Jake shrugged. They moved to the bar. Jake ordered a whisky, double, which meant he'd been here before and knew the measures were illegally small. He drank half the glass, looked around, and

Connections 8   THE GIFT OF TIME   Paul Stuart

said in a soft voice, "Normally, I wouldn't piss around with a stranger but I'm in a bind. I've got a thing going down and my man had to get out in a hurry. Now, here's the story. Joey Fadden-"

"I know him."

"I know you know Joey. That's why I'm here. Let me finish. Joey said you were solid, and I need somebody I can trust. Somebody from your line of work."

"Windows?"

"No. Don't be stupid. Your other line of work."

Ralston actually had two. One was washing windows. The other was breaking into houses and offices and walking off with anything he thought he could sell. Big difference. You have to know your distribution pipeline.

"And you understand that if we can't come to an agreement here and anything goes wrong later, either one of my boys or me will come to visit you."

It wasn't phrased as a question. The threat was like the fine print in a contract. It had to be included but nobody paid it much attention.

"Yes, yes. Fine. Go on."

"Let me explain. I heard from Joey about a month ago that this TV crew did a story. Life in prison or some shit like that. I don't know. The crew got to spend a great deal of time with the prisoners.

Connections 8   THE GIFT OF TIME   Paul Stuart

Why is it that such connections happen? There must be something about people on the outside wanting to feel a rapport with those inside. It always goes wrong when they find out what it's really like."

"Macho shit, sure." Ralston had seen it before.

"So, Joey heard them talking about this TV poker show some asshole producer is doing. It's planned for Mayfair in a hotel, not a real casino. And they don't use chips. They use real cash. The buy in's supposed to be 250k."

"Shit cash! What's the game?" Ralston loved poker.

"I don't know. Old Maid. Snap. Fish. I don't play cards. It's a mug's game. So I'm thinking, if it's not a casino security can't be very tight. Might be something to think about."

Jake ordered another whisky.

"Ok. So, I check out the prison show and get some names. And one of the gaffers..."

"What is that? I've heard of them."

"Electrician. Can I finish? He's a biker, too. And he's loose-mouthed when he's had a few. Which is often. So, I get the details. First of all, it's a live show."

"What's that mean?"

"Live? They don't record it ahead of time."

Connections 8   THE GIFT OF TIME   Paul Stuart

"They do that?" Ralston thought everything was recorded.

"So it's a big surprise who wins."

"That's not a bad idea for a show. I mean, I'd watch it."

Ralston peeled the label of his beer bottle. It was a nervous habit. Jake noticed him and stopped.

"Well, you can tell them you approve, or you can shut up and listen. You were given two ears and only one mouth for a reason. Think about it."

The insult went completely unnoticed.

Joey shrugged and continued. "My point is that they'll have a million and a half in small notes on the set. And we'll know exactly when and exactly where. So Joey speaks for you and I thought you might be interested. You want in, you get twenty."

"It's not a casino's money, but there'll still be armed guards."

"If there are guns involved, I'd be more interested for thirty."

"I could go to twenty-five."

Sammy Ralston said he'd have to think about it. That meant a phone call to Joey Fadden, who was doing time for armed robbery. By virtue of the circumstances, their conversation was convoluted, but the most important sentence was a soft, "Yeah, I know Jake. He's ok."

Connections 8   THE GIFT OF TIME   Paul Stuart

That settled it. They proceeded to talk about sport and the teams they supported.

Connections 8   THE GIFT OF TIME   Paul Stuart

-4-

The site of the game was the The Mayfair Arcadia. On Wednesday morning, the day of the show, the contestants assembled in one of the hotel's conference rooms. It was a curious atmosphere: the typical camaraderie of fellow performers, with the added element that each one wanted to take a large sum of cash from the others. The mix was eclectic.

Stone T, a hip-hop artist, whose real name, O'Connor learned from the biography that Feltham had prepared for the press, was Emmanuel Evan Jackson. He had been a choirboy in a city baptist church, had put himself through university, performing at night, and then he moved into the reap, ska and hip-hop scene, Stone was decked out in drooping jeans, Nikes, a vast sweatshirt and bling. All of which made it jarring to hear him say things like, 'It's a true pleasure to meet you. I've admired your work for a long time.' And: 'My wife is my muse, my Aphrodite. She's the one whom I dedicate all my songs to,'

O'Connor was surprised to see Brad Knightly was one of the contestants. He was widely known as a bad boy in the West End of London. The lean, intense-eyed kid was a pretty good actor in small roles, never with a major lead, but it was his

Connections 8 THE GIFT OF TIME Paul Stuart

personal life that had made the headlines. He'd been thrown out of clubs for fighting, had several arrests and he'd done time in jail for completely destroying a hotel room and giving the two security guards, who'd come to see what the fuss was about, a good kicking. He seemed cheerful enough at the moment, though, and was attentive to the emaciated blonde hanging on his arm, despite the fact that Andrew Feltham had asked that the contestants attend this preliminary meeting alone, without partners or spouses.

Knightly was unfocused and O'Connor wondered if he was stoned. He wore his hat backwards and the sleeves of his wrinkled shirt rolled up, revealing a tattoo that started with Gothic a letter F. The rest of the word disappeared underneath the sleeve but nobody doubted what the remaining letters were.

Sandra Glickman was the only woman in the game. She was originally from New York, but lived in London now. She worked at the Laugh Factory and Caroline's and appeared occasionally on Comedy Central on TV. O'Connor had seen her once or twice on TV. Her routines were crude and funny. ('Hey, you guys out there will be interested to know I'm bisexual; buy me something and I'll have sex with you.'). O'Connor had learned that she'd gone to

Connections 8   THE GIFT OF TIME   Paul Stuart

Harvard on a full scholarship and had a master's degree in advanced maths. She'd started doing the comedy thing as a lark before she settled down to teach maths or science. That had been six years ago and comedy had won over academia.

Charles Bingham was a familiar face on TV and movies, though few people knew his name. Extremely tanned, fit, in his early sixties, he wore a blue blazer and tan trousers, dress shirt and tie. His dyed blond hair was parted perfectly down the side and it was a fifty-fifty chance that it was a rug, O'Connor estimated. Bingham was a solid character player and that character was almost always the same: the older ex-husband of the leading lady, the co-worker or brother of the leading man, a petty officer in a war movie, and one of the first to get killed in battle.

He'd been born Charles Brzezinski, the rumour was. But so what? O'Connor's own first name was still legally Maurice.

The big surprise in the crowd was Dillon McKennah. The handsome thirty something was a big screen actor. He'd be the one real star at the table. He'd been nominated for an Oscar for his role in a Spielberg film and everybody was surprised he'd lost. He'd made some bad choices recently: lackluster teen comedies and a truly terrible horror

Connections 8   THE GIFT OF TIME   Paul Stuart

film in which gore and a crashing soundtrack substituted, poorly, for suspense. Even on his most depressed days, O'Connor could look at himself in the mirror and say that he'd never taken on a script he didn't respect. McKennah mentioned that he was working on a new project, though he gave no details. But every actor was engaged in a 'new project', just like every writer had a script 'in development.'

They drank coffee, ate from the luxurious spread of breakfast delicacies and chatted. As the conversation continued O'Connor was surprised to find how lucky he was to be there. Apparently, when word went out about the proposed new show, close to five thousand people had contacted Andrew Feltham's office, either directly or through their agents. It seemed that everybody wanted a part of the action.

Now, the door of the conference room swung open and Andrew Feltham entered.

"Okay. How is everybody? Ready to go? I saw your show last night," he said to the woman called Sandy.

"Were you that heckler? I should have had you thrown out!" she replied.

"I'm not that stupid. I would never spar with you like that."

Connections 8   THE GIFT OF TIME   Paul Stuart

"Hey, Andrew, can we drink? On the set I mean?" asked Brad Knightly. "I play better that way.

"You can do anything you want," Feltham told him, "but you pay for any breakages."

When the coffee cups were refilled and breakfast table raided again, Feltham sat on the edge of the table in the front of the room.

"Now, today's the day. I want to run through the plan. First, let's talk about the game itself."

He asked a young man into the room. The slim newcomer had been flown in from Las Vegas and he also sat down, before awing them with a display of his incredible dexterity. He then went through protocol and rules of the game they'd be playing.

"Texas Hold 'Em." He waited for reaction, but there was none. Everybody was in full concentration mode. This is one of the simplest of all poker games and had been chosen so the audience could follow the play.

"There is no ante; the players to the dealer's left place blind bets before the deal. This will be a small blind from the player to the dealer's immediate left and then a large blind, twice that amount, from the player on his left to create a pot. Each player will then be dealt two 'hole' cards, which nobody else can see, and then each places a bet or folds. The amount

Connections 8   THE GIFT OF TIME   Paul Stuart

of the blinds will be set before the game." The man paused to check that his audience was with him.

"Now comes the 'flop.' This is three cards dealt face-up in the middle of the table. Betting starts again and two more 'community' cards are dealt face-up, making five. Traditional rules of betting apply. You can check, call, raise or fold. Rounds of betting will carry on until we get to the showdown, when you use your two hole cards plus any three of the face-up cards to make the best hand you can. The player who has the best hand and has not folded by the end of all the betting rounds wins all the money in the pot."

The man stopped and looked at each player in turn, carefully and studiously making sure he was satisfied they each understood.

"One thing we're not doing," Feltham said, when he had left an appropriate silence, "there will be no hidden cameras." Feltham wanted the tension of live drama. "Where's the excitement if the audience knows what everybody's hand is? I want people at home to be on the edge of their seats. Actually, I'd prefer it if they fell off them! Also, please remember, you're on live TV. Don't pick your nose or scratch unfortunate places. And," he continued, "you'll be wearing microphones, so please watch your language. Even whispers will be picked up.

Connections 8   THE GIFT OF TIME   Paul Stuart

We'll bleep out your naughty words, but your mother will know. I want laughs and sighs and banter. We'll have three cameras on close-ups and medium angles and one camera on top showing the whole table. No sunglasses. We want to see your eyes. I want expression. Cry, look exasperated, laugh, get pissed off. This is a poker game but it's a TV show first and foremost. I want the audience engaged. Any questions?"

There were none and the contestants dispersed.

On his way to join Diane for a swim before the show, Mike O'Connor was trying to recall what was familiar about Feltham's speech. Then he remembered it was out of a gladiator film, when the man in charge gave his before-the- games pep talk, reminding the warriors that though most of them were about to die, they should go out and put on the best show they could.

Connections 8   THE GIFT OF TIME   Paul Stuart

-5-

Sammy Ralston and Jake were in a bar just around the corner from the hotel. It was chokingly hot.

"This is like Nevada," Ralston commented. "Why do they always put casinos where the weather's like this?"

Ralston was sweating. Jake wasn't, despite being much the larger and heavier man.

The biker said, "if the weathers 'nice people stay outside and don't gamble. If the weather's shitty, they stay inside and spend their money. It's not rocket science."

Ralston fed a pound coin into the mini-slot at the end of the bar and Jake looked at him wondering why he should throw his money away like that. Ralston lost and fed another pound in. He lost again. The two men had spent the last few days checking out the Mayfair venue. It was one of those places that dated from the fifties and was showing its age. It reminded Ralston of his grandmother's apartment décor. A lot of yellows, a lot of mirrors that looked like they had bad skin conditions and a lot of fading white statuettes.

Jake, with his tattoos and biker physique stood out

Connections 8   THE GIFT OF TIME   Paul Stuart

Big-time, so he'd done most of the behind the scenes information gathering, from press releases and a few discreet phone calls. He'd learned that the TV show would be shot in the Grand Ballroom. At the beginning of the show, armed guards would give each player a suitcase containing his buy-in, which would sit on a table behind his chair. He'd take what he needed from it to play.

"It'll be a big suitcase."

"No. Two fifty doesn't take up much room."

"Oh." Ralston supposed Jake would know this. The most he himself had ever boosted in cash was £2,000, but that was in coinage and he'd put his back out moving it from the arcade to his car.

After the initial episode tonight was over, the money went back into the suitcases of the players who hadn't gone bust. The guards would take it to the hotels safe for the night.

As for the surveillance of the casino, Ralston had done most of that. He had his window-washing truck and his gear there, so he was virtually invisible. All contractors were. He'd learned that the ballroom was in a separate building. The guards would have to wheel the money down a service walkway about sixty feet or so to get to the safe. Ralston found that the path was lined with tall plants, a perfect place to hide to jump out and

Connections 8   THE GIFT OF TIME   Paul Stuart

surprise the guards. They'd overpower, cuff and duct tape them, grab the cases and flee to the opposite car park.

He and Jake discussed it and they decided to act that night, after the first round of games. After the next finale on the next night there'd be more people around and they couldn't be sure if the money would be returned to the safe.

The plan sounded okay to both men, but Jake said, "I think we need some kind of, you know, distraction. These security people are pros. They're going to be everywhere."

Ralston suggested setting off some explosion on the grounds. Blow up a car or pull the fire alarm.

Jake didn't like that. "As soon as anybody hears that they'll know something's going down and the money will have guards all over it." Then he blinked and nodded. "Hey, you noticed people getting married around here a lot?"

"Yes, I have."

"And everybody getting their picture taken?"

Ralston caught on. "All those flashes. You mean blind them somehow?"

Jake nodded. "But if we walk up with a camera, the guards will freak."

"How about we get one of those flashes you see at weddings? The remote ones."

Connections 8   THE GIFT OF TIME   Paul Stuart

"Yeah. On tripods."

"We get one of those, set it up about halfway along the walkway. When they're nearby we flash it. They'll be totally blinded We come up behind. They won't know what hit them. I like it. Think we can find something like that around here?"

"Probably."

The men paid for their beers and stepped out into the heat.

"Oh, one thing. What about....you know?"

"No, I don't know until you tell me."

"A gun. I don't have a gun."

Jake laughed. "Have you ever used one?"

"Of course." In fact, that was a lie. He'd never fired a gun and he was annoyed that Jake seemed to be laughing at him about it.

When they were in the window washing truck, Jake grabbed his canvas backpack from behind the seat. He opened it up for Ralston to see. There were three pistols inside.

"Take your pick."

Ralston chose the revolver. It had fewer moving parts and levers and things on the side. With this one he wouldn't have to ask Jake how it worked.

Connections 8   THE GIFT OF TIME   Paul Stuart

-6-

The banquet hall where the show was being shot was huge and it was completely packed. The place was also decked out like every TV set that Mike O'Connor had ever been on: a very small portion, which is what the camera saw, was sleek and fashionably decorated. The rest was a mess of scaffolding, cameras, wires and lights. It looked like a factory.

The contestants had finished with hair and make-up and the sound man had wired them with mikes to their chests and plugs to their ears. They were presently in the greenroom, making small talk. O'Connor noted the clothes. Sandra Glickman was low-cut and glittery; Knightly was still in his hat-backward, show the tattoos mode. Stone T was subdued South London and had managed to get Feltham to agree to his wearing Ali G goggles. These were not nearly as dark as sunglasses; you could get a good look at his eyes (for the 'drama' when he won a big pot or ended up busted, presumably). Charles Bingham was in another blazer and razor creased grey trousers. He wore a tie. Dillon McKennah wore the de-rigeur costume of pretend youth, an untucked striped blue and white shirt over a black 't' shirt and tan chinos. His hair was spiked up in a fringe above his handsome face.
■■■

Connections 8   THE GIFT OF TIME   Paul Stuart

O'Connor had been dressed by Diane in 'older man sexy.' Black jacket, white 't' shirt, jeans and cowboy boots. 'Gunfight at the OK Corral,' she'd whispered and kissed him for luck.

The production assistant, who was young, brunette and nervous, stood in the greenroom's doorway, clutching a clipboard, a massive radio on her hip. She listened to the voice of the director from the control room and kept glancing at her watch.

Television was timed to the tenth of a second.

Suddenly she stiffened. "Okay everyone, please. We're on in three." She then rounded them up like cattle and headed them to the assembly point.

There, O'Connor looked at the monitor, showing what the viewers would be seeing: splashy graphics and some brash music. Then the camera settled on a handsome young man sitting at a desk, like a sports commentator.

"Good evening. I'm Lyle Westbrook, your host for *'Go For Broke.'* Two exciting days of no-holds-barred poker. And joining me here are Andy Brock, three times the winner of the World Championship of Poker in Atlantic City and Pete Bronsky, a professional gambler and author of 'Make a Living out of Playing Cards. This is reality TV at its most real. You're watching live, on location, six

Connections 8   THE GIFT OF TIME   Paul Stuart

individuals who are not playing for prestige, they are playing for a charity of their choice. They are playing with their own hard-earned cash. Somebody's going to win, maybe as much as six times that. One and a half million is going to be at play tonight. We can already feel the excitement and I can't imagine the tension our contestants must be feeling at this moment."

O'Connor tuned out of the banter, realizing that this was, in fact, the big time. Millions of people would be watching them and, more importantly, dozens of network and studio executives would be watching the ratings.

"And now, let's meet our contestants."

They went out in alphabetical order, as the announcer made a few comments about each of them and their careers. O'Connor caught Diane's eye as she sat in rapt attention in the front row. So close he could have touched her.

When they were all seated around the table, security guards brought in the cash, which had been transferred online to a local bank only a few hours before. The audience murmured when the guards, rather dramatically, opened the cases and set them behind each player on a low table. They stood back, scanning the audience from behind sunglasses.

Connections 8   THE GIFT OF TIME   Paul Stuart

O'Connor tried not to laugh at the exaggeration of the whole thing.

The dealer explained the rules again, for the audience, and then, with cameras hovering, sweat already dripping, the room went utterly silent. The dealer nodded to O'Connor to his immediate left, who pushed the agreed small blind of £1,000 onto the table. For the big blind, Knightly to O'Connor's left splashed the table, tossing the £2,000 out carelessly. This was very bad form and the others frowned in disapproval. He took no notice as the dealer straightened it.

The hole cards were dealt, the top card discarded and the flop cards spun elegantly into the centre of the table. The game proceeded with nobody winning or losing big, no dramatic hands. Knightly bet hard and took some losses, but then pulled back. Sandy Glickman, with the quick mind of a natural comedian and mathematician, seemed to be calculating the odds before each bet. She increased her winnings slowly. Stone T was a middle-of-the-road player, suffering some losses and catching some wins, as did McKennah. Neither seemed like natural players. O'Connor played conservatively and continually reminded himself of the basic poker strategy he'd had drilled into him by Diane in the last few weeks.

Connections 8   THE GIFT OF TIME   Paul Stuart

It's okay to fold up front. You don't have to play every hand. Bluff rarely, if at all. Bluffing should be used appropriately and only against certain players in limited circumstances. Many professional players go for months without bluffing. Fold if you think you're going to lose, no matter how much you've already put into the pot.

Always watch the cards. This version of poker is played with a single 52 card deck, and only seven cards are known to any one player: his two and the five community cards. Unlike counting cards at blackjack or baccarat, knowing those seven won't give you great insights into what the others have. But knowing the table, you can roughly calculate the odds of whether somebody else has a hand that beats yours.

Most important in poker, of course, is to watch the people playing against you. Some gamblers believe in identifying gestures or expressions that's suggest what people have as the hole cards. O'Connor didn't believe in 'tells' like scratching your eye when you have a high pair in the hole. He did know, however, that people respond consistently to stimuli. For example, Stone T's face grew still when he had a good, though not necessarily a winning, hand. File those facts away and be aware of them.

Connections 8   THE GIFT OF TIME   Paul Stuart

The game progressed, with Glickman and McKennah up slightly, Knightly, Stone and O'Connor down a bit. Bingham was the biggest loser so far. On The whole O'Connor was pleased with his performance. He was playing a solid game.

They took a commercial break and Feltham walked out, dispensing water and telling everybody how pleased he was and how favourable the initial responses were. He walked off stage and he heard the voice of God.

"Now, back to the action," the commentator said. Then silence. O'Connor and the others couldn't hear anything else from the host or the pros in the control room.

A new deal. The blinds were now increased to five thousand and ten thousand. The hole cards were dealt.

Shit.

O'Connor hoped he hadn't muttered that out loud. He had the worst hole cards that anyone could have, an unsuited two and a seven. You can't make a straight because you're allowed only three cards from the table, and there was no chance of a flush. There was a miraculous possibility for a full house but at best it would be sevens and twos. Not terrible, but still a long shot.
■■

Connections 8   THE GIFT OF TIME   Paul Stuart

He stayed in for one round of betting but Bingham and Glickman started raising each other. Knightly folded, spitting out a word that O'Connor knew would be bleeped out. McKennah folded and then O'Connor did too. He was mentally counting the money he had left, which was about £220,000, when he realised that something was going on at the table. Bingham, Glickman and Stone were engaged in battle. He sensed that Stone didn't have great cards but was already in for close to a hundred thousand. Glickman was less raucous than earlier, which told him that she might have a solid hand, and Bingham tried to appear neutral. He fondled the lapel of his jacket.

The flop cards were the jack of spades, king of diamonds, three of clubs, seven of clubs and the six of hearts.

The dealer raised an eyebrow in the direction of Sandra Glickman.

"Seventy-five thousand," she raised, sighing. "Think of all the eye-liner that could buy."

The audience laughed. In her comedy routines she was known for excessive make-up.

Stone sighed too. And folded.

Bingham took a peek at his own cards again. This was a bad sign. It meant that he was double checking to verify that he had one of the better

Connections 8   **THE GIFT OF TIME**   Paul Stuart

hands, such as a straight or a flush. Then he looked over his money. His suitcase was empty, and he only had about sixty-thousand on the table.

"All in," he said. Under standard rules of poker, he could call with less than the raise, but couldn't win more than what he'd put into the pot. O'Connor saw the older man's hands descend to his trousers. He wiped his sweaty palms. His face was still. All eyes were on the cards.

And the announcer said, "we'll be back for the conclusion of this exciting clash."

Agony. The next five minutes were agony.

The cards remained face down on the table. The contestants chatted and sipped water. Knightly told a filthy joke to Glickman, who was subdued for a change and she smiled distantly. If she lost this hand she wouldn't go bust, but would be way behind. If Bingham lost he'd be heading home.

Both Glickman and Bingham kept smiles on their faces, but you could see the tension they felt. Their overturned cards sat in front of them. The waiting was torture for O'Connor, and he had nothing to lose.

After an interminable few minutes the action returned to the table.

The dealer said, "Ma'am you've been called. Would you please show your cards?"

Connections 8   THE GIFT OF TIME   Paul Stuart

She turned her two over and revealed the full house.

Bingham smiled stoically. "Ah." He displayed the ace-high flush. She'd beaten him with one hand better than his.

He rose and gave her a kiss. Then shook hands with the others. The protocol was that anyone who went bust had to rise and leave. "The walk of shame." Departing this way seemed ignominious, but this wasn't just poker, it was the hybrid of poker on television. The security guard displayed the empty suitcase to the table and the camera and then deposited it in a specially built rubbish bin. Very dramatic.

The audience applauded enthusiastically as Sandy raked in her cash.

After a commercial break and the ceremonial opening of a fresh deck of cards, the play continued. The remaining players were warmed up now and the betting grew more furious. On the sixth hand of this segment, Glickman, O'Connor and McKennah all folded and Stone T and Knightly were left.

Then Stone T made a bad mistake. He tried to bluff. O'Connor knew you couldn't bluff against people like Knightly, either in poker or real life. People who trash hotel rooms and smack their girlfriends don't have anything to lose. They kept

Connections 8   THE GIFT OF TIME   Paul Stuart

raising hard and O'Connor could see that Stone was breaking the rule he'd been reciting to himself all night: don't stay in just because you've already spent money.

Stone pushed in the remaining stake of nearly eighty-thousand. He had a cool smile on his lips and terror in his eyes behind the Ali G lenses. Knightly took his time finishing his drink and then, with a sour smile, called his opponent.

Stone's two-pair hand was annihilated by an ace-high full house. One more contestant was gone.

There was time on that night's show for one more hand and it was during this round that divine retribution, in the form of Mike O'Connor, was visited upon Brad Knightly. It was really too bad, O'Connor reflected from the vantage point of someone who happened to have the best hand he'd ever had I his life; a straight flush, jack high. As the betting progressed and Glickman and McKennah dropped out, O'Connor assumed the same mannerisms he'd witnessed in Stone T when he was bluffing. Knightly was buzzed from the drink and kept raising, intent on bankrupting the old man. The odds were miniscule that Knightly had a better hand than his, so it seemed almost unfair to drive him out of the game so easily. But O'Connor was offended by Knightly's ego and childish behaviour, especially

Connections 8   THE GIFT OF TIME   Paul Stuart

after seeing the sneer on his face when he knocked Stone T out of the game. O'Connor wanted the upstart gone.

Which happened all of ten seconds later.

Knightly went all in and O'Connor turned the hole cards, his eyes boring into Knightly's, as if saying, "When I stay in a hotel, boy, I clean it up before I leave."

The audience applauded, as if the good gunslinger had just nailed the bad one.

Knightly grinned, drained his glass and took O'Connor's hand. He tried to clamp his hand hard, to show he still had strength, but that didn't work either. O'Connor smiled and slowly squeezed the hand hard enough to bring a wince to Knightly's face. He waited to release the hand until he was satisfied that people had noticed Knightly's discomfort and humiliation.

Then, the theme once again and the red eyes on the camera went dark. The show was over for the night. Exhausted and sweating, O'Connor said goodnight to the other players and the host. Andrew Feltham joined them. He was excited about the initial ratings, which were apparently even better than he'd hoped. Diane joined them. They all made plans to have dinner together in the resort's restaurant. O'Connor suggested that those who'd

Connections 8   THE GIFT OF TIME   Paul Stuart

lost should join them, but Feltham said they were being taken out to another restaurant by an assistant.

O'Connor understood. To the victor the spoils, even though it wasn't yet over. It was important to keep the buzz going and losers don't figure.

Diane said she'd meet them in the bar in twenty minutes. She headed off to the room and Feltham went to talk to the line producer, while O'Connor and McKennah signed some autographs.

"Let me buy you a beer, McKennah offered.

O'Connor accepted and they moved through the huge hall as the assistants took care of the equipment. TV and movies are as much about lights, electronics and computers as they about acting. The two security guards were assembling the suitcases of money.

"Where's the bar?" O'Connor asked.

"The main building I think," McKenna replied, looking around. "I think there's a shortcut. There's a walkway there."

"I need a drink," O'Connor said and they began their walk.

Connections 8   THE GIFT OF TIME   Paul Stuart

-7-

Sammy Ralston felt the pistol, hot and heavy, in his back waistband. He was standing in the bushes in dark overalls spearing litter and slipping it into a rubbish bag.

On the other side of the walkway, behind other bushes, waited big Jake. The plan was that when the guards wheeling the money from the ballroom to the motel safe were halfway down the walkway, Ralston would hit the switch and flash the powerful photographer's light, which was set up at eye level. They'd tried it earlier. The flash was so bright it had blinded him, even in the well-lit room, for a good ten or twenty seconds.

After the burst of light, Ralston and Jake would race up behind them, cuff the guards, then wrap duct tape around their mouths. With the suitcases of money, the men would return to the stolen van, parked thirty feet away, around the corner of the banquet facility. They'd drive a few miles away to Ralston's truck, then head back to California.

Ralston looked at his watch. The show was over and the guards would be packing up the money now. But where were they? It seemed to be taking a lot of time. Were they even coming this way?

Connections 8   THE GIFT OF TIME   Paul Stuart

He glanced towards the door, then he saw it open.

The problem was that it wasn't the guards at all. It was just a couple of men. A younger one in a striped shirt and an older one in a T shirt, jeans and jacket. They were walking along the path slowly, talking and laughing.

Behind them, the door opened again and the guards, two of them, big and armed, of course, were wheeling the cart containing the cash suitcases along the path. Shit. The two men in front were screwing it all up. How was he going to handle it? He crouched in the bushes, pulling the pistol from the pocket.

Connections 8   THE GIFT OF TIME   Paul Stuart

-8-

"Oh, watch it there." McKennah pointed to a thick wire on the ground. It was curled and O'Connor had nearly caught his foot. O'Connor paused and squinted at it. He glanced at McKennah. Ironically, they'd been talking about the paparazzi and how they'd stalk you, even lay booby traps to catch you in embarrassing situations.

"Damn, look." McKennah gave a sour laugh. He walked up to what the wire was attached to, a photographer's light, set up on a short tripod halfway along the path. Angrily he unplugged it and looked around, seeking the owners of the equipment.

"Maybe it's part of the show."

"Then Andrew should've told us."

"Oh, there're some guards." He nodded at the security detail with the money, behind them. "I'll tell them. Sometimes I get a little paranoid, I have to admit. But there are some crazy people out there."

Ralston had to do something fast. The two men had spotted the photoflash and, it seemed, had unplugged it. The guards were only about fifty feet behind. What the hell could he do? Without the flash there was no way they'd surprise the guards.

He glanced towards Jake, but he was hiding behind thick bushes and seem not to have seen. And

Connections 8   THE GIFT OF TIME   Paul Stuart

the two men were just standing beside the light, talking and waiting for the guards.

This was their only chance. Only seconds remained. Then an idea occurred to Ralston.

Hostage.

He'd grab one of the men at gunpoint and draw the guards' attention while Jake came up behind them. No. Better than that. He'd grab one and wound the other. That would show he meant business. The security guards would drop their guns. Jake could cuff and tape them and the two men would be away. Everybody would be so busy caring for the wounded man, he and Jake could get to their truck before anybody realised which way they'd gone.

He pulled on the ski mask and, taking a deep breath, stepped fast out of the bushes, lifting the barrel towards the older of the two men, the one in the T-shirt and jacket, who gazed at him in astonishment. He aimed at the man's knee and started to pull the trigger.

O'Connor gasped, seeing the small man materialize from the bushes and aim a gun at him. He raised a protective hand, as if that would be any use at all.

"No, wait!" he shouted.
■■

Connections 8   THE GIFT OF TIME   Paul Stuart

But just as the man was about to shoot, there came a flash of motion from his right, accompanied by a grunting gasp.

Dillon McKennah leapt forward and, with his left hand, expertly twisted away the pistol. With his right he delivered a stunning blow to the assailant, sending him staggering back, cradling his wrist. McKennah then moved in again and flipped the man over onto his front and knelt on his back, calling for the guards.

O'Connor glanced back at the sound of footsteps running towards the car park. "There's another one. That way!"

But the guards remained on the walkway, drawing their guns. One stayed with the money, looking around. The other ran forward, calling into his microphone. In less than ten seconds the walkway was filled with security guards and uniformed officers.

The assailant's mask was torn off, revealing an emaciated little man in his forties, eyes wide with fear and dismay.

O'Connor watched a phalanx of guards, surrounding the money from the show, wheeling the cart fast into the hotel. Yet more guards arrived. The officers who'd gone after the footsteps and just returned, reported that they'd seen no one, thought

Connections 8   THE GIFT OF TIME   Paul Stuart

a couple reported a big man had jumped into a van and sped off.

"Dark, that's about all they could tell. You gentlemen, ok?"

O'Connor nodded. McKennah blinked.

"Fine," was all he said.

Diane came running out and she hugged her husband, asking how he was.

"Fine. I'm fine. I'm not even shaken," he assured her.

A senior police officer arrived and supervised the arrest. When he had been apprised of the circumstances the sombre man shook his head. "It gives a new meaning to 'reality TV, doesn't it? Now, let's get your statements down."

-9-

Shaken Andrew Feltham walked into the bar and found O'Connor and Diane, McKennah and Glickman. He ordered a soft drink. Shaken though he was, it was not the time to be seen drinking alcohol.

"Jesus, how are you all?"

For a man who'd almost been shot, O'Connor admitted he was doing pretty well.

"It was my idea to use the cash. I thought it'd go better. It's my fault," Andrew Feltham said.

"You can hardly blame yourself for some madman, Andrew. Who was he?"

"Don't know yet. Got a history of petty theft, I'm told. He had a partner, but he got away."

They talked about the incident and O'Connor recounted McKennah's martial arts skills.

"Are you all still okay to continue with the show?" Feltham probed.

McKennah and Glickman said they were. O'Connor said, "of course," but then he caught something in the producer's eyes. "That's not what you're really asking, is it Andrew?"

A laugh. "Okay. What I want to know is if we go ahead with the show tomorrow, how are people going to react? I want your honest opinion. Should

Connections 8   THE GIFT OF TIME   Paul Stuart

we give it some time to calm down? The dust to settle?"

"Which people?" McKennah asked. "The audience?"

"Exactly. Are they going to think it's in bad taste? I mean somebody could have been badly hurt."

O'Connor laughed. "Excuse me, Aaron, but when have you ever known a TV show to fail because it's in bad taste?"

Andrew Feltham nodded and smiled.

The Thursday finale of *'Go For Broke'* began with a brief description of the events of the previous night. That was wasted time, really, because every channel had covered it ad nauseam for the last few hours. There can't have been many people in the country who didn't know about it in great detail.

With the same fanfare as the previous day, and five sunglass-wearing guards nearby, the play among the last three contestants began. They played for some time without any significant changes in their positions. Then O'Connor got his first good hole cards of the night. An ace and jack, both spades.

The betting began. O'Connor played it with caution, though, checking at first then matching the other bets and raising slightly.
■■■

Connections 8   THE GIFT OF TIME   Paul Stuart

The flop cards were another ace, a jack and a two, all varied suits.

Not bad, he thought.

Betting continued, with both Glickman and McKennah now raising significantly. Though he was uneasy, O'Connor kept a faint smile on his face as he matched the hundred thousand bet by McKennah.

The fourth card, the turn, went face-up smoothly onto the table under the dealer's skillful hands. It was another two.

Glickman eyed both of her opponents' piles of cash. But then she held back, checking. That could have meant a weak hand or it was a brilliant strategy if she had a really strong one.

When the betting came to McKennah he slid out fifty thousand. O'Connor raised another fifty. Glickman hesitated and then matched the hundred with a brassy laugh.

The final card went down. It was an eight. This meant nothing to O'Connor. His hand was set. Two pair, aces and jacks. It was a fair hand, but hardly a guaranteed winner. But they'd be thinking he had full house, aces and twos, or maybe even a four of a kind, in twos.

They, of course, could have powerful hands as well.

Connections 8 THE GIFT OF TIME Paul Stuart

Then Glickman made her move. She pushed everything she had left into the middle of the table.

After a moment of debate McKennah folded.

O'Connor glanced into the brash comedian's eyes, took a deep breath and called her, counting out the money to match the bet.

If he lost he'd have about fifty thousand to call his own and his time on the show would be over.

Sandy Glickman gave a wry smile. She slid her cards face down into the pile of discarded cards. She said, for the microphone, "Not many people know when I'm bluffing. You've got a good eye." The brassy woman delivered another message to him when she leaned forward to embrace him, whispering, "You shafted me and you didn't even buy me dinner."

It was quiet enough that the censors didn't need to hit their magic button.

But she gave him a warm kiss and a wink before she headed off down the Walk of Shame.

Connections 8   THE GIFT OF TIME   Paul Stuart

-10-

About twenty minutes remained for the confrontation between the last two players, O'Connor with £623,000 and McKennah with £877,000.

The young actor was to the dealer's left. He slid in the agreed small blind, ten thousand, and O'Connor counted out the big blind of £20,000.

As the dealer shuffled expertly the two men glanced at each other. O'Connor's eyes conveyed a message. You're okay and you saved my skin yesterday, but this is poker and I wouldn't be honest to myself, to you, or the game if I pulled back.

The deals continued for a time, with neither of them winning or losing big. McKennah tried a bluff and lost. O'Connor tried a big move with three of a kind and got knocked out by a flush, which he should have seen coming.

A commercial break and then, with minutes enough for only one hand, the game resumed. A new deck of cards was shuffled. McKennah put in the small blind bet. The rules now dictated twenty-five thousand at this point, and O'Connor himself put in fifty.

Then the deal began.

O'Connor kept his surprise off his face as he glanced at the hole cards, a pair of kings.

Connections 8   THE GIFT OF TIME   Paul Stuart

Okay, not bad. Let's see where we go from here.

McKennah glanced at his own cards without emotion. And his pre-flop bet was modest under the circumstances, fifty thousand.

Keeping the great stone face, O'Connor pushed in the same amount. He was tempted to raise, but decided against it. He had a good chance to win but it was still early and he didn't want to move too fast.   The dealer burned the top card and dealt the flop. First, a two of hearts, then the four of hearts and then the king of spades.

Suddenly, O'Connor had three of a kind, with the other two table cards yet to come.

McKennah bet fifty thousand. At this point, because he himself had upped the bet, it wouldn't frighten the younger player off for O'Connor to raise him. He saw the fifty and raised by another fifty.

Murmurs from the crowd.

McKennah hesitated and saw O'Connor. The turn card, the fourth one, wasn't helpful to O'Connor, the six of hearts. Perhaps it was useless to McKennah as well. He checked.

O'Connor noted the hesitation of the man's betting and concluded he had a fair, but unspectacular, hand. Afraid to drive him to fold, he bet only fifty thousand again, which McKennah saw.

Connections 8   THE GIFT OF TIME   Paul Stuart

They looked at each other over the sea of money as the fifth card, slid out. It was a king.

As delighted as O'Connor was, he regretted that this amazing hand, four of a kind, hadn't hit the table when more people were in the game. It was likely that McKennah had a functional hand at best and that there there'd be a limit to how much O'Connor could raise before his opponent folded.

As the next round of betting progressed, they put another hundred and fifty thousand into the pot. Finally, concerned that McKennah would sense his over confidence, O'Connor decided to buy time. "Check." He tapped the table with his knuckles.

A ripple went through the audience. Why was he doing that?

McKennah looked him over closely. Then said, Five hundred K."

And pushed the bet out.

The crowd gasped.

It was a bluff, O'Connor thought instantly. The only thing McKennah could have that would beat O'Connor was a straight flush. But, as Diane had made him learn over the past several weeks, the odds of that were very small.

O'Connor said in a matter of fact voice, "all in," pushing every penny of his into the huge pile of

Connections 8   THE GIFT OF TIME   Paul Stuart

cash on the table, nearly a million and a half pounds.

"Gentlemen, please show your cards."

O'Connor turned over his kings and the crowd erupted in applause. And they then fell completely silent when McKennah turned over the modest three and five of hearts to reveal his inside straight flush.

O'Connor let out a slow breath, closed his eyes momentarily and smiled.

He stood and, before taking the Walk of Shame, shook the hand of the man who'd just won himself one hell of a lump of money.

Connections 8   THE GIFT OF TIME   Paul Stuart

-11-

The weeks that followed the airing of the show were not the best of O'Connor's life. The loss of a quarter of a million pounds hurt more than he wanted to admit.

More troubling, he thought he'd get some publicity. But in fact there was virtually none whatsoever. He got some phone calls, but they were mostly about the foiled robbery and the rescue. He eventually stopped returning the reporters' calls.

He was left puttering around the house and playing a little golf.

And then one day, several weeks after the poker show, he happened to be playing couch potato and watching a World War Two adventure film from the sixties. He remembered having seen it as a boy. He'd loved it then and he still loved it. But now he realised there was something about it that he'd missed. He sat up and remained riveted throughout the film. Long after the film finished he continued to sit and think about it. He realised that he could identify with the people in the movie. Eventually, he rose.

Connections 8   THE GIFT OF TIME   Paul Stuart

-12-

"Hey, Mike. How're you doing? I'm sorry it didn't work out. That last hand. Phew. That was a cliff-hanger."

"I saw the ratings," O'Connor said to Andrew Feltham.

"They weren't bad."

Not bad? No, O'Connor thought, they were over the top amazing.

"So." Silence rolled around for a moment. "What are you up to next?"

Feltham was pleased to see him, but his attitude said that a deal was a deal. O'Connor had taken a chance and lost, and the rules of business meant that he and his producer's arrangement was now concluded.

"Taking some time off. Doing some writing."

"Ah, good. You know what goes around comes around."

O'Connor wasn't sure that it did. Or even what the hell the phrase meant. But he smiled and nodded.

Silence, during which the producer was, of course, wondering what exactly O'Connor was doing here.

Connections 8   THE GIFT OF TIME   Paul Stuart

"Let me ask you a question, Andrew. You like old films, right? Like your dad and I used to talk about."

Another pause. Feltham glanced at the spotless glass frames of his posters covering the walls. "Sure. Who doesn't?"

A lot of people didn't, O'Connor was thinking. They liked modern films. Oh, there was nothing wrong with that. In fifty years people would be treasuring some more modern movies. Every generation ought to like its own darlings best.

"You know, I was thinking about the show and guess what it reminded me of?"

"Couldn't tell you."

"A movie I just saw on TV."

"Really? About a poker showdown? An old western?"

"No. 'The Guns of Navarone." He nodded at the poster to O'Connor's right.

"Our show reminded you of that?"

"And that's not all. It reminded me of 'The Magnificent Seven, The Wild Bunch, The Dirty Dozen, Top Gun, Saving Private Ryan, Alien. In fact, a lot of films. Action films."

"I don't follow, Mike."

"Well, think about it. Formula. You start with a group of diverse heroes and send them on a

Connections 8   THE GIFT OF TIME   Paul Stuart

mission. One by one they're eliminated before the big last scene. In 'The Guns of Navarone,' for example. A group of intrepid commandos. Eliminated one by one, but in a certain order. Sort of reverse order of their youth or sex appeal. The stiff white guy's one of the first to go. Anthony Quayle in 'The Guns of Navarone, or Robert Vaughn in 'The Magnificent Seven. Next we lose the minorities. Yaphet Kotto in 'Alien.' Then the hothead young kid is bound to go. Shouldn't he have ducked when he was facing down the Nazi with the machine gun? I would have. But, no, he just kept going until he was dead."

"That brings us to women. If they're not the leads, they better be careful. Tyne Daly in one of the 'Dirty Harry' films. And even if they survive, it's usually so they can hang on the arm of the man who wins the showdown. And who does that bring us to finally? The main opponents? The white guy versus the enthusiastic young white guy. Tom Cruise versus Nicholson. Denzel Washington versus Gene Hackman. Clint Eastwood versus Lee Van Cleef, DiCaprio versus all the first class passengers on Titanic."

"Kind of like the contestants on the show. Stodgy white guy, minority, hot-headed youth, the woman. Bingham, Stone, Knightly, Sandy. And after

Connections 8 THE GIFT OF TIME Paul Stuart

they were gone, who was left? Old me versus young Dillon McKennah."

"I think you're pissed off about something, Mike. Why don't you just tell me?"

"The game was rigged, Aaron. I know it. You wrote your own 'reality' show like it was a classic Hollywood western or war movie. You knew how it was going to come out from the beginning. You followed the formula perfectly."

"And why would I do that?"

"Because I think you're trying to get a movie financing package with Dillon McKennah. That caper film he was talking about."

Feltham was speechless for a moment. Then he looked down. "We talked about a few things, that's all. Dillon and me. Oh, come on Mike. Don't embarrass yourself. It was just a reality show with a difference. There was no guarantee of a bump."

"But it did get Dillon a bump. A big one. And you know why? Because of the robbery. The more I thought about it, the more I realised it that was a classic Act Two reversal – according to the formula of scriptwriting. You know how that works. Big plot twist three-quarters of the way through. 'Guns of Navarone'? The young Greek girl, Gia Scala, the supposed patriot, turns out to be a traitor. She destroys the detonators. How are the commandos

Connections 8   **THE GIFT OF TIME**   Paul Stuart

going to blow up the German guns now? We're sitting on the edge of our seats, wondering."

"What does that have to do with anything?"

"The robbery, Andrew. The attempted robbery. It was all set up, too. You arranged the whole thing. That's what made it more than boring reality TV. My God, you even got the attempt and Dillon's Steven Segal karate moves on security camera and that night it was on You Tube and every network you can think of. TV at its best. You think there wasn't a human being in the country who wasn't going to turn on the second episode and watch Dillon and me slug it out?"

"I don't know what..."

O'Connor held up a hand. "Now, don't embarrass yourself, Andrew. I've talked to a friend of mine, a detective. He's retired now, but I trust his judgement. I told him I had a problem. I needed to know some facts about the case. He made some calls. First of all, the gun that Sammy Ralston had? It was a fake gun. From a studio property department. The sort they use on TV sets. Second, turns out that his phone records show Ralston called a prisoner, Joey Fadden, a few weeks ago. The same prisoner that you interviewed as part of a TV series about our prisons last year. I think you paid Joey to get Ralston's name. No, let me finish, it gets

Connections 8   THE GIFT OF TIME   Paul Stuart

better. Third, Ralston keeps talking about a mysterious biker named Jake who put the whole thing together and nobody knows about."

"Jake."

"I dug up a fake police badge and went to the bar where Ralston said he met with Jake. I had a photo with me."

"A...."

"It was a picture of you and your assistant. The big one. The bartender recognized him. You got him to play the role of Jake. Costume, fake tattoos, the whole thing. I just walked past his office, by the way. There are posters on his wall, too. One of them is 'Brokeback Mountain.' Starring Jake Gyllenhaal. Jake. Think about it."

Feltham said nothing, but his expression said it all.

"Dillon knew about the set up. He knew about the fake gun. That's why he took on a guy who was armed. He wasn't in any danger. It was all planned. All planned for the bump.

O'Connor shook his head. "I should have guessed before. I mean, the final hand, Andrew? You know how most poker games end: two guys half comatose from lack of sleep, and one beats the other with three sixes over a pair of threes. A four of a

Connections 8   THE GIFT OF TIME   Paul Stuart

kind versus a straight flush? That only happens in the movies. That's not real life."

"How could I rig the game?"

"Because you had an artist as the dealer. You saw his card tricks when we met him. I found him. I've got his name and address. Oh, and I also got the phone number of the gaming commission in Nevada, and the British authorities as well."

The man closed his eyes. Maybe he was thinking of excuses and explanations. O'Connor almost hoped he'd say something, because his reply would have been "save it for the judge."

But Feltham didn't try to excuse himself. He looked across the desk, as if it were a poker table, and then he said, "so, where do we go from here?"

"To put it in terms of television, Andrew," Mike O'Connor said, pulling several thick envelopes out of his briefcase, "let's make a deal."

Connections 8   THE GIFT OF TIME   Paul Stuart

SPLIT SECONDS COUNT

Olympic stadia are unlike any other structures on earth. From the 1936 sports complex in Berlin right through to the present day all exude true magnificence and each is a testament to a pivotal moment in human history.

The power, though, derives less from architecture than from the spirit of competitions past and those to come, an energy filling the massive spaces like the cries of spectators. An Olympic stadium is where you test yourself against your fellow man. For that defines human nature.

This philosophical thought was going through the mind of Yuri Umarov as he gazed at the world's most recent Olympic stadium, brilliantly conceived to resemble a bird's nest, its image rippling in the heat.

Yuri, sitting, coated in sweat, beside the track of a Beijing high school, where, along with dozens of other people, both local and international, he'd been training all morning.

Competition. Winning. Bringing glory to your country and its people. He felt this spirit now, this energy.

Though he felt exhausted as well. And the glory he sought seemed extremely elusive. His legs and side hurt from pounding along the track for the

Connections 8   THE GIFT OF TIME   Paul Stuart

hundredth time since 5am. His lungs hurt from inhaling the thick air. The government here had supposedly been working to cleanse the atmosphere, but to Yuri, a country boy from the mountains, it was like training in a roomful of smokers.

He looked up and saw his mentor approach.

Gregor Dallayev, white haired, twice his age, walked briskly. Still athletic himself, the man, who sported a massive moustache, was wearing white trousers and a dark shirt with a collar. Sweat stains blossomed under his arms, but he appeared otherwise unmoved by the fierce summer heat.

He was also unmoved by Yuri's performance.

"You are sitting down," Gregor said impatiently in Russian.

Yuri stood immediately. He took the water the man held and drank half down, then poured the rest on his head and shoulders. He was breathing harder than he needed to, trying to convince the older man that he was truly exhausted. Gregor's sharp eye studied the athlete with a look that said, "don't try to fool me. I've seen that before."

"That last run was unacceptable." He held up a stopwatch. "Look at the time."

Sweat clouded Yuri's eyes and he could hardly see the watch itself, much less the numbers.

Connections 8   THE GIFT OF TIME   Paul Stuart

"I was...."Yuri was going to come up with an excuse, a cramp, an obstacle on the track, but Gregor would not accept excuses from anyone. And in fact they tasted bad in Yuri's mouth, too. Such was his upbringing and training, during his nineteen years of life. "I'm sorry."

Gregor, though, relented, smiling. "The sun. It's not like home."

"No, sir. It's not like home at all."

Then, as they walked back towards the starting line, Gregor was once again the taskmaster. "Do you know what your problem is?"

There were undoubtedly many of them. Yuri found it easier to say, "No, sir."

"You are not seeing the second ribbon."

"The second ribbon?"

Gregor nodded. "In there," he said, nodding at the stadium sitting in the hazy sun, "in there, the best runners will not be running to break the tape with their chests at the finishing line."

"They won't?"

"No!" the mentor scoffed. "They will not even see the tape. They won't even see the finishing line. They will be concentrating on the second ribbon."

"Where is the second ribbon, sir?"

"It is beyond the finishing line. Maybe ten feet, maybe twenty. Maybe one."

Connections 8   THE GIFT OF TIME   Paul Stuart

"I don't think I've ever seen it."

"You don't see it, not with your eyes. You see it in here." He touched his chest. "In your heart."

Yuri waited for him to finish, as he knew the older man would.

"That is the ribbon you must reach. It's the goal beyond the goal. See, inferior runners will slow as they approach the end of the race. But you won't You will continue to go faster and faster, even though you can go no faster. You must pass through the finishing line as if it's not there and fly straight to the second ribbon."

"I think I understand, sir."

Gregor looked at him closely. "Yes, I think you do. Tomorrow, any time over thirty seconds is failure. Your whole journey here will have been wasted. You don't wish to disgrace yourself and your country, do you?"

"Of course not, sir."

"Good. Let's try it again. Your last run was thirty-one point two seconds. That's not enough. Now, take your mark. And this time, run for the second ribbon."

Billy Savitch was the youngest on the American team. In his thin running suit, emblazoned with the US flag, he was wandering

Connections 8   THE GIFT OF TIME   Paul Stuart

around the American compound, nodding hello to the athletes he knew, pausing to chat with the staff. And ignoring the flirts from the girls. Billy had no interest in them, but you could understand why they'd smile his way. He was rugged and handsome and charming. With his crew cut and sharp eyes and chiseled face he looked like a cowboy, and in fact, hailed from Texas.

This was the second time he'd been out of the country and the first time to the Olympics, though, of course, he watched the games every four years. The last time was with his wife and baby daughter.

And, my God, just think about it. Here he was in China, part of the most famous sporting event of the world. It was the best thing that had happened to him, apart from being a husband and father.

Though there was a bit of a taint on the experience.

His junior status. He was just a green kid. And, as an all-star running back on his team at home, it was hard for him to be relegated to the bottom of the barrel. Not that his colleagues didn't treat him politely. It's just that they rarely even noticed him.

Tomorrow was the start of the games and he knew he would be virtually ignored.
■■■

Connections 8   THE GIFT OF TIME   Paul Stuart

He shouldn't complain. But he was ambitious and had a restless streak about him. That was what had driven him there in the first place. Doing what he believed he was meant to do.

He lifted the bottle of water to his lips and drank a huge amount. He looked at his watch. In half an hour he could get into the gym and work out. He was looking forward to it. He'd worked out for two hours yesterday and he'd worked out for two hours again today. His arms were solid steel, his legs, too.

"Savitch!"

He turned immediately, hearing the voice of the man who was responsible for his being there.

Muscular and with a narrow, etched face, Frederick Alston strode quickly over the grass. That was one thing about him. He never made you come to him. He had that kind of confidence. He could walk right up to you and you'd still feel you'd been summoned. Despite the heat, he wore a suit and tie. He always did. Whatever the weather or the occasion.

Alston stopped and looked him over. The young man didn't expect a long conversation; that wasn't Alston's way. While some directors here would micromanage and look over the shoulder of

Connections 8   THE GIFT OF TIME   Paul Stuart

their teams, Alston didn't. If you couldn't pull your share, you were out. Just like that.

And in fact this encounter was brief.

What did surprise Billy, however, was the content of the short exchange. Actually, 'shock' would be a more apt description.

"I think you're ready to go on the field. Are you?"

Ready to what?"

"Are you ready to go on the field?" Alston repeated, seemingly irritated that he had to do so.

"Yessir."

"Good. Tomorrow. Nine a.m."

Opening day?" Billy blurted.

Alston's mouth tightened. "When is opening day?"

"Tomorrow."

"Then I guess that's what I mean." He started away. Then stopped. "One thing, Savitch?"

"Yessir?"

"Don't screw up."

"No, sir."

And with that his only advice, Alston turned, walking away briskly, leaving the young man standing beside a practice track, sweating in the sunlight as strong and hot as anything Texas had ever produced.

■■■

Connections 8   THE GIFT OF TIME   Paul Stuart

Ch'ao Yuan was in his forties, a solid man with gelled hair, cut short. He was wearing a dark suit and white shirt. He was a government bureaucrat, former Communist Party official, and presently head of security at the stadium. He was one of six such security officers who between them were in control of the various Olympic venues around the city. His was the most prestigious, he knew. And the most stressful. The big bird nest would be *the* target for enemies, of which his country had more than a few.

Not to mention the Israelis and Americans and Iranians. And the Iraqis....Oh, please.

Now, late afternoon before the first day of the games, he was sitting in a modest room in one of the many temporary office buildings constructed for the Olympics. He hadn't realised how much paperwork could be generated by a sporting event.

He was sitting forward, looking over his computer on which was a decrypted e-mail, which had been sent to him from an internal intelligence contact. He'd read it once. And now he was reading it again.

Trying to work out where this fell on the scale of dangers.

Connections 8   THE GIFT OF TIME   Paul Stuart

Security was, of course, intense. There were a number of systems in place. A security fence perimeter around the stadium. Passes with computer chips embedded in them. Fingerprint detectors, iris scanners. Metal detectors, of course, as well as bomb sniffers both canine and mechanical at entryways. Alarms on all the service doors. Automatic backup generators that took only thirty seconds to kick in and could support the entire power requirements of the stadium. And there were backups to those.

Ch'ao had five hundred security officers at his disposal. He was confident of the protective measures that had been taken. And yet, this particular piece of intelligence bothered him more than the others.

He grimaced and when his secretary announced that his visitors had arrived, he shut the computer screen off.

A few minutes later two men entered his office: Frederick Alston, whose American team was nearby, and his Russian counterpart, Vladimir Rudenko, whose team was some miles away.

He'd met them weeks ago and they'd become friends despite their different cultures and histories. 'Strange bedfellows' was the expression that Alston had used.

Connections 8   THE GIFT OF TIME   Paul Stuart

He greeted them in what was the virtual if not official language of the Olympics, English, though both Alston and Rudenko said 'hello' in passable Mandarin.

Ch'ao said, "I must tell you something. I've received a communication of a security threat against either of your teams, or both."

"Just Russian or American?" Rudenko asked.

"That's right."

"From the Arabs?" Alston asked. He had short grey hair and smooth skin, which pock-marked Ch'ao envied.

"No information about the source of the threat."

Rudenko, a large but spongy man, who stood out in contrast to the lean and muscular athletes he came to China with, gave a faint laugh. "I wouldn't bother to ask about us. The motherland has far too many enemies."

"What's the threat?" Alston asked.

"Not really a specific threat. It's a tip off."

"Tip," Alston corrected.

"Yes," Rudenko added. "A tip off is what happens in basketball, one of our favourite sports." His wry look to Alston meant only one thing: a reminder of the famous 1972 game and Russia's controversial win. Alston ignored the dig.

Connections 8 THE GIFT OF TIME Paul Stuart

Ch'ao continued, explaining that an informant said he'd seen someone in a green Chevy taking delivery of plastic explosives yesterday. "And another informant, independent of the first, said that there was going to be an attempt to target some of your players here. I don't know if they're related but it would seem so."

"Green what?" Rudenko asked. "Cherry?"

Ch'ao explained about the inexpensive car that was sweeping the country.

"And you don't know more than that?"

"No, we're checking it out now."

The Russian chuckled. "And there's a look in your eye, may I say Comrade Ch'ao, that makes me concerned."

Ch'ao sighed and nodded. "I'm asking you to pull your teams from tomorrow's competition until we see what's going on."

Rudenko stared. Alston laughed. "You can't be serious."

"I'm afraid so."

"It's the opening day of the games. We have to compete. It would look very bad if we didn't.

"Yes, and some of these players are here for only one or two events. If they don't play tomorrow, they might lose their only chance of a lifetime to compete in the Olympics."

Connections 8   THE GIFT OF TIME   Paul Stuart

"Our young men and women have trained for this for years."

"I understand the dilemma, but I'm concerned for the safety of your players."

The Russian and American looked at each other. Alston said, "I'll talk to the team. It will be their decision. But I can tell you right now how they'll vote."

"How many threats like this have you received? Rudenko asked.

"We've received dozens of threats. Nothing this specific, though."

"But, the Russian pointed out, "That's hardly specific."

"Still, I must strongly suggest you consider withdrawing."

The men said their goodbyes and left the office.

An hour later Ch'ao's phone rang. It was Alston explaining that he'd talked to everyone on the team and the decision was unanimous. They would compete. We're here to play. Not to hide."

He'd no sooner finished the call from the Russian, saying that his team, too, would be participating on opening day.

Sighing, Ch'ao hung up thinking: No wonder the Cold War lasted so long, if the Kremlin and

Connections 8   THE GIFT OF TIME   Paul Stuart

White House back then were like these two – stubborn and foolish as donkeys.

Around 9 a.m. on the first day of the games a man cycled up to a low dusty building near Chaoyang Park, which was, coincidentally, a venue for one of the events: the volleyball competition. The man paused, hopped off and leaned his bike against the wall. He looked up the street, filled with many such bicycles, and observed the park, where security officers patrolled.

He kept his face emotionless but, in fact, he was incensed that the Chinese had won the Olympics that year. Furious. The man was a Uighur, pronounced Wee-Gur. These were a Turkic speaking people from the middle of China, who had long fought for their independence, mostly politically but occasionally through terrorism.

He took a pack of cigarettes from his shirt pocket and slipped his stubby fingers inside. He found the key that had been hidden there when he was secretively palmed the pack and, looking around, undid a padlock on the large door, pulled it open and stepped inside.

There he found the green car, one of the small new ones that were flooding China. He resented the car as much as the Olympics because it represented

Connections 8   THE GIFT OF TIME   Paul Stuart

more money and trade for the country that oppressed his people.

He opened the boot. There he found several hundred posters, urging independence for the Uighur people. They were crude but they got the point across. He then opened another box and examined the contents, which excited him much more than the Mao-style rhetoric: Thirty kilos of a yellow, clay-like substance, which gave off a pungent aroma. He stared at the plastic explosives for a long moment, and then put the lids back on the boxes.

He consulted the map and noted exactly where he was to meet the man who would supply the detonators. He started the car and drove carefully out of the warehouse, not bothering to close and lock the door. He also left his bicycle behind. He felt a bit sad about that having had it for a year, but, considering the direction his life was about to take, he certainly wouldn't need it any longer.

"Look at you," said Gregor, eying his young protégé's training jacket, a Russian flag bold and clear on the shoulder. From a young age Yuri had been taught not to pay too much attention to his appearance, but today he'd spent considerable time, after warming up, of course, shaving and combing his hair.

Connections 8   THE GIFT OF TIME   Paul Stuart

The teenager smiled shyly, as Gregor saluted.

They were outside the stadium, near a security fence, watching the thousands of spectators head in serpentine lines towards the stadium. Near the two men, buses continued to disgorge the athletes as well, who were walking through their own entrance with their gear bags over their shoulders. Some were nervous, some jovial. All were eager.

Gregor consulted his watch. The Russian team would be taking pictures with the heads of the Olympic committee in half an hour's time, just before the games began. Yuri would, of course, be there, front and centre. "You should go. But first...I have something for you."

"You have, sir?"

"Yes."

Gregor reached into his pocket and pulled out a small bag. He extracted a gold coloured strip of satin.

"Here, this is for you."

Yuri exclaimed, "It's the second ribbon!"

Gregor was not given to soft expressions of face but he allowed himself a faint smile. "It is indeed." He took it from the boy, tied a knot and slipped it over his neck.

"Now go and make your country proud."

Connections 8   THE GIFT OF TIME   Paul Stuart

"I will, sir."

Gregor turned and stalked off in that distracted way of his, as if you'd slipped from his mind the instant he turned. Though Yuri knew that was never the case.

The Uighur found the intersection he'd sought and parked the green car. Ahead of him, a mile away, he could see part of the Olympic stadium. It did indeed look like a bird's nest.

For vultures, he thought. Pleased with his cleverness.

Ten minutes until the man was to meet him there. He was Chinese and would be wearing black trousers and a yellow Mao jacket. The Uighur scanned the people walking by on the streets. He hated it in Beijing. The sooner.....

His thoughts faded as he saw motion in the rearview mirror. Police were running towards him pointing.

They were not your typical Beijing police, nor Olympic guards in their powder blue uniforms. These were military security, in full battle gear, training machine guns his way. Shouting and motioning people off the street.

No! I've been betrayed! He thought.

He reached for the ignition.

Connections 8   THE GIFT OF TIME   Paul Stuart

Which was when he and the car vanished in a fraction of a second, becoming whatever a boot full of plastic explosives turns you into.

Yuri Umarov cringed like everyone else around him, when the bang came from somewhere south of the stadium. The decorative lights around the stadium went out. A few car alarms began to bleat. And Yuri began to run.

He hurdled the security fence but the guards were, like everyone else, turning towards the explosion, wondering if a threat would follow from that direction.

Then he hit the ground in the secure zone and began running towards the stadium, sprinting for all he was worth, pounding along the concrete, then the grass.

Thirty seconds.

That was all the time, his mentor Gregor had told him, that he would have to sprint to the back of the stadium and open it up before the emergency generators kicked in and the alarm systems went back online.

Breath coming fast, a machine gun firing, rocks avalanching down a mountain. His lungs burned. Counting the seconds: twenty-two, twenty-one.

Connections 8   THE GIFT OF TIME   Paul Stuart

Not looking at his watch, not looking at the guards, the spectators. Looking at only one thing; something he couldn't even see. The second ribbon.

Eighteen seconds, seventeen.

Faster, faster.

The second ribbon.

Eleven, ten, nine....

Then, sucking in the hot, damp air, sweat streaming, he came to the service door. He ripped a short crowbar from his pocket, prised the door open and leapt into the cold, dim storeroom inside the belly of the stadium.

Six, five, four.....

He slammed the door shut and made sure the alarm sensors aligned.

Click.

The lights popped back on. The alarm system glowed red. He said a brief prayer of thanks.

Yuri crouched, stretching his agonized legs, struggling to breathe in the musty air around him.

After five minutes he rose and stepped to one of the interior doors, which weren't alarmed, and he entered the brightly lit corridor. He made his way past the shops and stands. He finally stepped outside the stadium itself, which opened below him.

It was magnificent. He was chilled at the sight. People were once more streaming into the stadium,

Connections 8   THE GIFT OF TIME   Paul Stuart

apparently reassured by an announcement that the brief power outage was due to a minor technical difficulty.

Laughing to himself at the comment, Yuri orientated himself. He found the place on the stadium grounds, at the foot of the dignitaries' boxes, where the Russian team was milling about, awaiting their photo session with officials.

Wonderful, he reflected. And there was also a CCTV camera. God willing, it would be a live transmission and would broadcast throughout the world his shout, "Death to the Russian oppressors! Long live the Republic of Chechnya!"

He'd rehearsed the cry as many times as he had practiced his thirty-second run. Now, Yuri knelt and unzipped his sports bag. He began slipping the detonator caps into the explosives inside and rigging them to the push-button detonator. Sprinting full out from the security fence to the stadium with the bomb armed was, as Gregor had pointed out, not a good idea.

"What was it?" Ch'ao Yuan demanded, speaking into his mobile phone.

"We aren't sure, sir."

"Well, somebody is sure," Ch'ao snapped.

Connections 8   THE GIFT OF TIME   Paul Stuart

Because that somebody, from the public liaison office, had gone onto the public address system to tell 85,000 people that there was no risk. It was a technical problem and it had been resolved.

Yet nobody had called Ch'ao to tell him anything.

One of his underlings, a man who spoke mandarin as if he'd been raised in Canton, was continuing. "We've checked with the state power company. We can't say for certain, sir. The infrastructure....you know. This has happened before. Overuse of electricity."

"So you don't know if it was a bomb or it was the half-million extra people in the city turning on their air conditioning."

"We're looking now. There's a team there, examining the residue. They'll know soon."

"How soon?"

"Very soon."

Ch'ao slammed the phone shut. He was about to make another call when a man walked into his office. Ch'ao rose. He said respectfully, "Mr Liu."

The man, a senior official from internal security in Beijing, nodded. "I'm on my way to the stadium, Yuan."

Ch'ao noted the dismissive use of his first name.
■■■

Connections 8   THE GIFT OF TIME   Paul Stuart

"Have you heard?"

"Nothing yet, sir."

Liu, a long face and bristly hair looked perplexed. "What do you mean?"

"About the explosion, I assume. Nothing. The men are still searching the relay station. It will be..."

No, no, no." The man's expression was explosive. He gestured broadly with his hands. "We have our answer."

"Answer?"

"Yes. I have my people there now. And they've found Uighur independence posters. The terrorist was on his way to the stadium when we found him on a tip. The bomb detonated prematurely as he was being arrested."

"Uighur?" This made some sense. Still, Ch'ao added, "I wasn't told."

"Well, we're not making the information widely available as yet. We think he was going to drive the car into the crowd at the entrance. But he saw the police and detonated the bomb where it was. Or the system malfunctioned."

"Or perhaps there was some gunfire." Ch'ao was ever vigilant about being respectful. But he was furious at this peremptory disposition of the case. Furious, too, that, whatever the cause of the explosion, there was no witness to interrogate. And

Connections 8   THE GIFT OF TIME   Paul Stuart

everyone knew the military security forces were quick to pull the trigger.

But Liu said calmly, "There were no shots." He lowered his voice. "If the mechanism was constructed here, a malfunction is the most likely explanation." He actually smiled, "So the matter is disposed of."

"Disposed of?"

"It's clear what happened."

"But this could be part of a broader conspiracy."

"When do the Uighurs have broad conspiracies? They are always one man, one bomb, one bus. No conspiracy, Yuan."

"We have to investigate. Find out where the explosives came from. Where the car came from. The informant said the targets were the Russians or the Americans. There was no mention of the Uighurs."

"Then the informant was wrong. Obviously."

Before thinking, Ch'ao blurted, "we must postpone the games."

"What are you talking about?"

"Until we find out more."

"Postpone the games? Are you a madman, Yuan? We were presented with a threat. We have met that threat. It is no longer a threat." Liu often spoke as he were reading from old-time propaganda.

Connections 8   THE GIFT OF TIME   Paul Stuart

"You're satisfied that there's no risk, sir?"

"The reserve generators are working, are they not?

"Yes, sir."

"All the security is in place and no one was admitted through the metal detectors until the power resumed, correct?"

"Yes, sir, Though the systems were down for a full thirty seconds."

"Thirty seconds," Liu mused. "What can happen in that time?"

Nowadays, 85,000 people can die, Ch'ao thought. But he could see Liu was not pleased with his attitude. He remained silent.

"Well, there we are. If something else turns up, we will have to consider it. For now, the explosion was infrastructure. This evening we will announce the bombing was the result of the Uighur movement. We'll say that there was no intent to harm anyone; the explosion was meant to be an inconvenience." Liu's eyes grew focused and dark. "And you will say nothing for the time being except infrastructure. An overloaded electrical system. After all, we still have a few things left to blame the Chairman for."

■■

Connections 8   THE GIFT OF TIME   Paul Stuart

There was a fortunate development, Yuri noted, his bag over his shoulder, as he trooped down the endless steps towards the field.

He observed a number of American athletes were standing near the Russians, chatting and laughing.

This was perfect. The Americans had offered only lip service to the Chechen plight, being far more interested in foreign trade with Russia. In fact, back in Grozny, planning the attack, Gregor told him, they'd considered targeting Americans too, but a dual attack was considered too difficult.

But now, Yuri was thrilled to see, he would take a number of the citizens of both countries to the grave with him.

He nodded at a guard, who gave him the most perfunctory of glances at his pass and motioned him on. Yuri stepped onto the Olympic field and made his way towards the two teams. In his mind was a vision of the second ribbon.

Standing on the grass grounds of the Olympic field, Billy Savitch looked around him. The field had been impressive when he'd seen it upon arrival. It was even more so now.

He was near a group of American athletes. He nodded greetings. They gave him thumbs up and

Connections 8   THE GIFT OF TIME   Paul Stuart

high fives. I'm actually on the field, he reflected. The first day of the games. And then he recalled, "don't screw up."

I'll try. No, trying is what losers do. I won't screw up.

The Americans were next to a large group of Russians. Most of the team, it seemed. They were waiting to have their picture taken by a Chinese photographer. There was also a media crew and an interpreter; they were doing interviews with certain athletes.

Billy stayed close to the Americans, many of whom were walking over to their Russian competitors and shaking hands. Wishing them luck, but always keeping that certain ruthlessness of eye. He wondered if he, too, looked ruthless.

He heard the announcer repeat that the power failure had been due to a technical problem. The evasive language of all governments. They apologized for the inconvenience.

A Russian nodded to him and said to a lean US athlete nearby, "What's your event, my friend?"

"I am a sprinter," the American said.

"A sprinter?" The Russian looked at him with a gaze of wistfulness. "I envy that. You are a hawk. Me, a plodding ostrich! I run long distances. When do you compete?"

Connections 8   THE GIFT OF TIME   Paul Stuart

"In an hour."

"You must be impatient."

"Yeah, some. But this isn't about me. It's about the team."

The Russian laughed. "Spoken like a good communist."

The two men laughed.

Billy joined them as he viewed another Russian athlete, slim with thick slicked-back hair, walking towards them from the stands, his bag over his shoulder. He had a pleasant smile on his face as he surveyed the field around him. He headed straight for the Russians at the photography station.

"Where are you from?" the first Russian asked Billy. "Your voice."

"Texas."

"Ah. The stars at night." The man clapped his hands four times, drawing another laugh from Billy.

One of the Russian coaches announced something. Presumably it was time for the sprinters because the men and women began clustering around the photographer. The long-distance runner said, "Come with me, my cowboy friend. You and your colleague. I want you both in the picture, too."

"Us?" Billy asked.

The man's eyes sparkled. "Yes, so you'll have something to remember our victory over you."

Connections 8   THE GIFT OF TIME   Paul Stuart

Yuri was twenty feet away from the dignitary box, which was draped in red in honour of the host country, a and blue and white in honour of the birthplace of the games. He noted that the photographer was set up and a number of Americans were mingling with the Russians. Young men and women, happy to be there, thrilled.

If they only knew what the next few minutes would bring. A shattering explosion, ball bearings and nails tearing skin, piercing their highly tuned bodies.

He looked around. There were guards in the stands and some near the doors, but none close enough. He was, as the Americans said, home free.

When he was ten feet away he'd detonate the device, he decided. That would be plenty close enough. He swung the bag under his arm and began to unzip and pull out the detonator.

As he was doing this, he glanced at someone nearby, looking at him, someone with the American team, wearing running gear. He was a young man, blond. He was rubbing his crew-cut head.

But not only rubbing his head, Yuri realised to his shock. He was speaking into a microphone on the inside of his wrist.

His eyes met the blond American's.

Connections 8   THE GIFT OF TIME   Paul Stuart

Yuri froze. Then frantically began to reach into his bag for the detonator button. That was the exact moment that the young American drew a pistol from his jacket, and aimed at Yuri's head. People screamed and dived for the ground.

Yuri went for the button. He saw a flash, but not from the explosive. It was from the hand of the young American.

And then he saw nothing.

Frederick Alston and Billy Savitch were standing in the office of Security Chief Ch'ao.

Billy thought he looked a little like Jackie Chan, but he didn't think it would be a good idea to say that. You had to be careful about accidental insults in China, he'd learned.

"I'm so very grateful to you both," Ch'ao said, rising and clasping their hands in both of his.

Billy nodded, looking like the bashful southern boy that he was. Secretly he, too, was grateful. As the junior member of the US State Department Security Team, which Alston headed, he had never expected to be on the front line of an operation in Beijing. He'd expected he'd continue to do what he'd been doing since arriving: checking IDs, standing on rooftops with a machine gun, checking cars, sweeping bedrooms.

Connections 8   THE GIFT OF TIME   Paul Stuart

But Alston had had enough confidence in Billy to put him to work in the stadium.

"How did you know that man was a terrorist?" Ch'ao asked him.

"I didn't, not at first. But I've studied all the entrances and exits of the stadium, and players were never in the part of the stands where he was coming from. You can't get to that place from the competitors' entrance. Why would he come from that direction? And he was carrying his sports bag. None of the other players on the field had bags; they were all in the locker rooms." Billy shrugged. "Then I looked into his eyes. And I knew."

"Who was he?" Alston asked.

"Yuri Umarov. Lived outside of Grozny. He came into Beijing with Gregor Dallayev last week. They've been training ever since, making the bomb, surveying the grounds and security.

"Dallayev, sure." Alston nodded. "The separatist guerilla. We think he was involved in the Moscow subway attack."

"We'll be able to find that out for certain," the Chinese man said with a smile. "He's in custody."

Billy asked, "What was their plan exactly?"

Ch'ao explained, "they made connections with a cell of Uighur terrorists and promise them thirty kilos of plastic explosive to use as they wished, as

Connections 8   THE GIFT OF TIME   Paul Stuart

long as it disrupted the games. A Uighur picked up the explosives at a drop site near Chaoyang Park this morning. It was that green Chevrolet I told you about. He drove to a meeting place not far from the stadium. We think that he believed he was meeting an intermediary to pick up the detonators. But the explosive was already rigged to blow remotely. We had that tip early about explosives in a green car."

"Which Gregor called in?" Alston asked.

"Yes, I'm sure. So as soon as the Uighur parked near the electrical relay station Gregor made the anonymous call and reported the green car. When the police arrived, Gregor blew the car up with a remote control and that took out the power station next to it."

"So that was the point of meeting there," Alston said. "A cover to take out the electricity."

"That's right. It shut down the alarm system temporarily and gave Yuri the chance to get inside."

Alston added, "we heard from Washington that your government wanted to end it right there, with the Uighur's death. But you called us to say there was more of a threat. How did you know that?"

"Just like you," a nod at Billy Savitch, "I didn't know, but I suspected. I play 'Go'. Do you know it?"

"Never heard of it," Billy said. Alston, too, shook his head.

Connections 8   THE GIFT OF TIME   Paul Stuart

"It's our version of chess. Only better, of course." He didn't seem to be making a joke. "I look forward when I play the game. You must always look forward to beat your opponent at 'Go'. You must see beyond the board. Well, I looked forward today. Yes, the explosion could have been an accident. But looking forward, I believed it could be an excellent diversion."

His phone buzzed. There was a rattle of Chinese. Ch'ao grimaced. Said something back and ended the call.

"Something wrong?" Aslton asked.

"I would like to ask a favour."

"OK."

"There will be a man here in a few minutes. His name is Mr. Liu. He....well, shall I say, he is not a forward thinker. I promised him that I would not alert the security forces there might be another threat."

"Politics, eh?"

"Precisely."

"Fine with us." He looked at Billy. "Savitch here acted on his own initiative."

"Yes, sir."

"Thank you."

Then in the distance a huge round of cheering and applause rose from the bird nest.

Connections 8   THE GIFT OF TIME   Paul Stuart

Ch'ao looked at his watch and then consulted the programme. "Ah, the first events are over. They're awarding the medals. Let me find out the results." He made a call and spoke in that explosive way of his. He nodded, then finished the call.

"Who won the gold?" Billy asked.

Ch'ao only smiled.

Connections 8   THE GIFT OF TIME   Paul Stuart

A WEEK IN TIME

MONDAY

"A new weapon."

The slim man in a conservative suit eased forward and lowered his voice. "Something terrible. And our sources are certain it will be used this coming Saturday morning. They're certain of that."

"Four days," said retired Colonel James J. Peterson, his voice grave. It was now 5 p.m. on Monday.

The two men sat in Peterson's nondescript office, in a nondescript building. There is a misconception that national security operations are conducted in high-tech bunkers filled with sweeping steel and structural concrete, huge screens ten feet high and attractive boys and girls dressed in designer clothes. That's what TV demands and we, by and large, accept it.

This place, on the other hand, looked like an insurance agency.

The skinny man, who worked for the government, added, "we don't know if we're talking conventional, nucular or something altogether new. Probably mass destruction, we've heard. It can do quote 'significant' damage."
■■■

Connections 8   THE GIFT OF TIME   Paul Stuart

Despite using the word 'nuclear' virtually every day of his working life, the skinny man shared the incorrect pronunciation with many people, including newsreaders and high-up politicians. It sounded somewhat ridiculous to the sharp listener.

"Who's behind this weapon? The Koreans? Iranians? ISIS? Al-Qaeda? Russians?"

"One of our enemies, and we seem to have quite a list at the moment. That's all we know at this point, so we need to find out about it. Money is no object, of course."

"Any leads?"

"Yes, a good one. An Algerian who knows who formulated the weapon. He met with them in Tunis last week. He's a professor and journalist."

"Terrorist?"

"He doesn't seem to be. His writings have been moderate in nature. He's not openly militant, but our local sources are convinced he's had contact with the people who created the weapon and plan to use it."

"You have a picture?"

A photograph appeared as if by magic from the slim man's briefcase and slid across the desk like a lizard.

Colonel Peterson leaned forward.

Connections 8   THE GIFT OF TIME   Paul Stuart

TUESDAY

Chaabi music drifted from a nearby café, lost intermittently in the sounds of trucks and scooters charging frantically along the commercial streets of Algiers.

The driver of the white van, a swarthy local, stifled a sour face when the music changed to Western Rock. Not that he actually preferred the old-fashioned, melodramatic chaabi tunes or thought they were more politically or religiously correct than Western music. He just didn't like Britney Spears.

Then the big man stiffened and tapped the shoulder of the man next to him, an American. Their attention swung immediately out of the front window to a curly haired man in his thirties, wearing a light coloured suit, walking out of the main entrance of the Al-Jazier School for Cultural Thought.

The man in the passenger seat nodded. The driver called, "ready," in English and then repeated the command in Berber-accented Arabic. The two men in the back responded affirmatively.

The van, a battered Ford, sporting Arabic letters boasting of the city's best plumbing services, eased forward, trailing the man in the light suit. The driver had no trouble moving slowly without being

Connections 8   THE GIFT OF TIME   Paul Stuart

conspicuous. Such was the nature of the traffic here in the old portion of the city, near the harbour.

As they approached a chaotic intersection, the passenger spoke into a mobile phone. "Now."

The driver pulled nearly even with the man they followed, just as a second van, dark blue, in the oncoming lane, suddenly leapt the kerb and slammed directly into the glass window of an empty storefront, sending a shower of glass onto the pavement as bystanders gaped and came running.

By the time the crowds on Rue Ahmed Bourzina helped the driver of the blue van extricate his vehicle from the shattered shopfront, the white van was nowhere to be seen.

Neither was the man in the light suit.

WEDNESDAY

Colonel James Paterson was tired after the overnight flight from Dulles to Rome, but he was operating on pure energy.

As his driver sped from Da Vinci Airport to his company's facility south of the city, he read the extensive dossier on the man whose abduction he had just engineered. Jacques Bennabi, the journalist and part time professor, had indeed been in direct communication with the Tunisian group that had

Connections 8   THE GIFT OF TIME   Paul Stuart

developed the weapon, though Washington still wasn't sure who the group was exactly.

Peterson looked impatiently at his watch. He regretted the day-long trip required to transport Bennabi from Algiers to Gaeta, south of Rome, where he'd been transferred to an ambulance for the drive. But planes were becoming too closely regulated for comfort. Peterson had told his people they had to keep a low profile. His operation, south of Rome, was apparently a facility that specialize in rehabilitation services for people injured in industrial accidents. The Italian government had no clue that it was a sham, owned ultimately by Peterson's main company: Intelligence Analysis Systems.

IAS was like hundreds of small businesses throughout the United States that provided everything from copier toner to consulting to computer software to the massive US government.

IAS, though, didn't sell office supplies.

Its only product was information, and it managed to provide some of the best in the world. IAS obtained this information not through high-tech surveillance but, Peterson liked to say, the old-fashioned way.
■■■

Connections 8   THE GIFT OF TIME   Paul Stuart

One suspect, one interrogator, one locked room. It did this very efficiently. And completely illegally. IAS ran black sites.

Black site operations are very simple. An individual with the knowledge the government wishes to learn is kidnapped and taken to a secret and secure facility outside the jurisdiction of the United States. The process is known as extraordinary rendition. Once at a black site the subject is interrogated until the desired information is learned. And then he's returned home. In most cases, that is.

IAS was a private company, with no official government affiliation, though the government was, of course, its biggest client. They operated three sites: one in Bogota, Columbia, one in Thailand, and the one that Peterson's car was now approaching. This was the largest of the IAS sites, a nondescript beige facility whose front door stated, "Funzione Medica Di Riabilitazione."

The gate closed behind him and he hurried inside, to minimize the chance that a passerby might see him. Peterson rarely came to the black sites himself, because he met regularly with government officials and it would be disastrous if anyone connected him to an illegal operation like this. Still, the impending threat of the weapon dictated that he

Connections 8 THE GIFT OF TIME Paul Stuart

personally supervise the interrogation of Jacques Bennabi.

Despite his fatigue, he got right to work and met with the man waiting in the facility's windowless main office upstairs. He was one of several interrogators that IAS used regularly, one of the best in the world, in fact. A slightly built man, with a confident smile on his face.

"Andrew," Peterson nodded in greeting using the pseudonym the man was known by. No real names were used in black sites. Andrew was a US soldier on temporary leave from Afghanistan.

Peterson explained that Bennabi had been carefully searched and scanned. They found no GPS chips, listening devices or explosives in his body. The colonel added that sources in North Africa were still trying to find whom Bennabi had met with in Tunis, but were having no luck.

"Doesn't matter," Andrew said, "I'll get you everything you need to know soon enough.

Jacques Bennabi looked up at Andrew. The soldier returned the gaze with no emotion, assessing the subject, noting his level of fear. A fair amount, it seemed. This pleased him. Not because Andrew was a sadist, he wasn't, but because fear is a guage to a subject's resistance.
■■■

Connections 8   THE GIFT OF TIME   Paul Stuart

He assessed that Bennabi would tell him all he wanted to know about the weapon within four hours.

The room in which they sat was a dim, concrete cube, twenty feet on each side. Bennabi sat on a metal chair with his hands behind him, bound with restraints. His feet were bare, increasing his sense of vulnerability, and his jacket and personal effects were gone because they gave subjects a sense of comfort and orientation. Andrew pulled a chair close to the subject and sat.

Andrew was not a physically imposing man, but he didn't need to be. The smallest person in the world need not even raise his voice if he has power. And Andrew had all the power in the world over his subject at the moment.

"Now," he said in English, which he knew Bennabi spoke fluently, "as you know, Jacques, you're many miles from your home. None of your family or colleagues knows you're here. The authorities in Algeria have learned of your disappearance by now. We are monitoring that. Do you know how much they care?"

No answer. The dark eyes gazed back, emotionless.

"They don't. They don't care at all. We've been following the reports. Another university professor

Connections 8   THE GIFT OF TIME   Paul Stuart

gone missing. So what? You were robbed and shot. Or the Jihadi Brothership finally got round to settling the score for something you said in class last year. Or maybe one of your articles upset some Danish journalist, and they kidnapped and killed you." Andrew smiled at his own cleverness. Bennabi made no reaction. "So, no one is coming to help you. You understand? No midnight raids. No cowboys riding to the rescue."

Silence.

Andrew continued, unfazed. "Now, I want to know about this weapon you were discussing with your Tunisian friends." He was looking carefully at the eyes of the man. Did they flicker with recognition? The interrogator believed they did. It was like a shout of acknowledgement. Good.

We need to know who developed it, what it is and who it's going to be used against. If you tell me you'll be back home in twenty-four hours." He let this sink in. "If you don't, things won't go well."

The subject continued to sit passively. And silently.

That was fine with Andrew; he hardly expected an immediate confession. He wouldn't want one, in fact. You couldn't trust subjects who caved in too quickly.

Connections 8   THE GIFT OF TIME   Paul Stuart

Finally, he said, "Jacques, I know the names of all your colleagues at the university and the newspaper where you work."

This was Andrew's talent. He had studied the art of interrogation for years and he knew that people could much more easily resist threats to themselves than to their friends and family. Andrew had spent the past two days learning every fact he could about people close to Bennabi. He'd come up with lists of each person's weaknesses and fears. It had been a huge amount of work.

Over the next few hours Andrew never once threatened Bennabi himself, but he was ruthless in threatening his colleagues. Ruining careers, exposing possible affairs, questioning an adoption of a child and even suggesting that some of his friends could be subject to physical harm.

A dozen specific threats, two dozen, offering specific details; names, addresses, offices, cars they drove, restaurants they enjoyed.

But Jacques Bennabi said not a word.

"You know how easy it was to kidnap you," Andrew muttered. "We plucked you off the street like picking a chicken from a street vendor's cage. You think your friends are any safer? The men who got you are back in Algiers, you know. They're ready to do what I say."

Connections 8   THE GIFT OF TIME   Paul Stuart

The subject only stared back at him.

Andrew grew angry for a moment. He cleared his raw throat and left the room. Had a drink of water, struggled to calm down.

For three more hours he continued the interrogation. Bennabi paid attention to everything said, it seemed, but he said nothing.

"Hell, he's good," Andrew thought, struggling not to reveal his own frustration. He glanced at his watch. It had been nearly nine hours, and he hadn't uncovered a single fact about the weapon.

Well, it was time to get serious now. He scooted his chair even closer.

"Jacques, you're not being helpful. And now, thanks to your lack of co-operation, you've put all your friends at risk. How selfish can you be?" he snapped.

Silence.

Andrew leaned close. "You understand that I've been restrained, don't you? I had hoped you'd be more co-operative, but apparently you're not taking me seriously. I think I have to prove to you how grave this matter is."

He reached into his pocket. He pulled out a printout of a computer photograph that had been taken yesterday. It showed Bennabi's wife and children in front of their home outside Algiers.

Connections 8   THE GIFT OF TIME   Paul Stuart

THURSDAY

Colonel Peterson was in his hotel room in the centre of Rome. He was awoken at 4 p.m. by his secure mobile phone.

"Yes?"

"Colonel." The caller was Andrew. His voice was ragged.

"So, what'd he tell you?"

"Nothing."

The colonel muttered, "you just tell me what he said and I'll figure out if it's important. That's my job." He clicked the light on and fished for a pen.

"No, sir, I mean he didn't say a single word."

"Not a ....word?"

"Over sixteen hours. Complete silence. The entire time. Not one word. Never happened in all my years in this business."

"Was he getting close to breaking, at least?"

"I....no, I don't think so. I even threatened his family. His children. No reaction. I'd need another week. And I'll have to make good on some of the threats."

But Peterson knew they were already on shaky ground by kidnapping somebody who was not a known terrorist. He wouldn't dare kidnap or endanger the professor's colleagues, let alone his family.

Connections 8 THE GIFT OF TIME Paul Stuart

"No," the colonel said slowly, "That's all for now. You can get back to your unit. We'll go to phase two."

The woman was dressed conservatively, worked with women at the university and had actually written in favour of women's rights. Peterson decided to use Claire for the second interrogator. Bennabi would view her as an enemy, yes, but not as inferior. And, since, it was known that Bennabi had dated and was married, with several children, he was clearly a man with an appreciation of attractive women. And Peterson knew that Claire was certainly that.

She was also an army captain, in charge of a prisoner of war operation in the Middle East, though at the moment she, too, was on a brief leave of absence to permit her to practice her own skills as an interrogator. Her skills were very different from Andrew's but just as effective in the right circumstances.

Peter now finished briefing her. "Good luck," he added.

And he couldn't help reminding her that it was now Thursday and the weapon would be deployed the day after tomorrow.

Connections 8   THE GIFT OF TIME   Paul Stuart

In perfect Arabic, Claire said, "I must apologise, Mr. Bennabi. Jacques. May I use your first name?" She was rushing into the cell, a horrified look on her face.

When Bennabi didn't reply, she switched to English, "Your first name? You don't mind do you? I'm Claire. And let me offer you my deepest apologies for this terrible mistake."

She walked behind him and took the restraints off. There was little risk. She was an expert at aikido and tae kwondo and could easily have defended herself against the weak and exhausted subject.

But the slim man, eyes dark from the lack of sleep, face drawn, simply rubbed his wrists and offered no threatening gestures.

Claire pressed the button on the intercom. "Bring the tray in, please."

A guard wheeled it inside: water, a pot of coffee and a plate of pastries, which she knew from the file, Bennabi was partial to. She sampled everything first, to show nothing was spiked with poison or truth serum. He drank some water but when she asked, "Coffee? Something to eat?" he gave no response.

Claire sat down, her face distraught. "I'm so terribly sorry about this. I can't begin to describe

Connections 8   THE GIFT OF TIME   Paul Stuart

how horrified we are. Let me explain. Someone, we don't know who, told us that you met with some people who are enemies of our country." She shifted her hands.

"We didn't know who you were. All we heard was that you were sympathetic to those enemies and that they had some plans to cause huge destruction. Something terrible was going to happen. Imagine what we felt when we heard you were a famous professor, and an advocate of human rights! No, someone gave us misinformation about you. Maybe accidental." She added coyly, "Maybe they had a grudge against you. We don't know. All I can say is we reacted too quickly. Now, first, let me assure you that whatever threats Andrew made, nothing has happened or will happen to your colleagues or family. That was barbaric what he suggested. He's been disciplined and relieved of duty."

No response whatsoever.

Silence filled the room and she could hear only her heartbeat, as she tried to remain calm, thinking of the weapon and the hours counting down until it was used.

"Obviously this is a very awkward situation. Certain officials are extremely embarrassed about what's happened and are willing to offer, what we could call, reparation for your inconvenience."

Connections 8   THE GIFT OF TIME   Paul Stuart

He continued to remain silent but she could tell he was listening to every word.

"Mr. Bennabi, Jacques, I have been authorized to transfer one hundred thousand pounds into an account of your choice. That's tax free money, in exchange for your agreement not to sue us for this terrible error."

Claire knew he made thirty-five thousand per year as a professor and journalist.

"I can order it done immediately. Your lawyer can monitor the transaction. All you have to do is sign a release agreeing not to sue."

Silence.

Then she continued with a smile, "And one more small thing. I myself have no doubt you have been wrongly targeted but, the people who have to authorize the payments want to be reassured that the meeting was innocent. I know it was. If I had my way I'd press a button and transfer the money right now, but they control the money." A smile. "It's just the way the world works, I suppose."

Bennabi said nothing. He stopped rubbing his wrists and sat back.

"They don't need to know anything sensitive. Just a few names, that's all. Just to keep the money men happy."

Connections 8 THE GIFT OF TIME Paul Stuart

Is he agreeing? She wondered. Is he disagreeing? Bennabi was different from anybody she's ever interrogated. Usually by now, subjects were already planning how to spend the money and telling her whatever she wanted to know.

When he said nothing she realised that he was negotiating.

A nod.

"You're a smart man. I don't blame you one bit for holding out. Just give us a bit of information to verify your story and I can probably go up to a hundred and fifty thousand."

Still no response.

"I'll tell you what. Why don't you name a figure? Let's put this all behind us." Claire smiled again, "we're on your side, Jacques. We really are."

FRIDAY

At 9.a.m. Colonel Jim Paterson was in the office of the rehabilitation centre, sitting across from a large, dark skinned man, who'd just arrived from Darfur.

Akhem asked, "What happened with Claire?"

Paterson shook his head. "Bennabi didn't go for the money. She sweetened the pot up to a quarter of a million." The colonel sighed. "Wouldn't

Connections 8   THE GIFT OF TIME   Paul Stuart

take it. In fact, he didn't even say no. He didn't say a word. Just like with Andrew."

Akhem took this information with interest but otherwise unemotionally, as if he were a surgeon called in to handle am emergency operation that was routine for him but that no one else could perform. "Has he slept?"

"Not since yesterday."

"Good."

There was nothing like sleep deprivation to soften people up.

Akhem was of Middle Eastern descent, though he'd been born in America and was a US citizen. Like Paterson, he'd retired from the military. He was now a professional security consultant; a euphemism for mercenary soldier. He was here with two associates, both from Africa. One was white, one black.

Paterson had used Akhem on half a dozen occasions, as had other governments. He was responsible for interrogating a Chechen separatist to learn where his colleagues had stashed a busload of Moscow schoolchildren last year. It took him two hours to learn the exact location of the bus, the number of soldiers guarding them, their weapons and pass codes.
■■

Connections 8   THE GIFT OF TIME   Paul Stuart

Nobody knew how he'd done it and no one wanted to.

Paterson wasn't pleased he'd had to turn to Akhem's approach to interrogation, known as extreme extraction. Indeed, he realised that the Bennabi situation raised the textbook moral question on using torture. You know a terrible event is about to occur and you have a prisoner in custody who knows how to prevent it. Do you use torture or not?

There were those who said no, you don't. That it's better to be morally superior and to suffer the consequences of letting the event occur. By stooping to the enemy's level and using their techniques it is said that the war is automatically lost, even if a military victory is gained.

Others said that it was our enemies who'd changed the rules; if they tortured and killed innocents in the name of their causes we had to fight them on their own terms.

Paterson had now made the second choice. He prayed it was the right ne.

Akhem was looking at the forage of Bennabi in the cell, slumped in a chair, his head cocked to one side. He wrinkled his nose and said, "three hours at the most"
■■

Connections 8 THE GIFT OF TIME Paul Stuart

He rose and left the office, gesturing his fellow mercenaries after him.

But three hours came and went. Jacques Bennabi said nothing, despite being subjected to one of the most horrific methods of extreme extraction.

In waterboarding, the subject is inverted on his back and water poured into his nose and mouth, simulating drowning. It's a horrifying experience, and also one of the most popular forms of torture because there's no lasting evidence, provided, of course, that the victim doesn't in fact drown, which happens occasionally.

"Tell me!" Akhem raged as the assistants dragged Bennabi to his feet, pulling his head out of the large tub. He choked and spat water from under the cloth mask he wore.

"Where is the weapon?" "Who is behind it? Tell me."

Silence, except for the man's coughing and spluttering.

Then to the assistants: "Again."

Back he went onto the board, his feet in the air. And the water began to flow once more. Four hours passed, then six, then eight.

Himself drenched, physically exhausted, Akhem looked at his watch. It was now early

Connections 8   THE GIFT OF TIME   Paul Stuart

evening. Only five hours until Saturday, when the weapon would be deployed, and he hadn't learned a single fact about it. He could hardly hide his astonishment. He'd never known anybody to hold out for this long. That was amazing in its own right. But more significant was the fact that Bennabi had not uttered a single word the entire time. He'd groaned, he'd gasped, he'd choked, but not a single word of English, Arabic or Berber had passed his lips.

Subjects always begged and cursed and lied or offered partial truths to get the interrogators to pause for a brief moment.

But not Bennabi.

"Again," Akhem announced.

Then, at 11 p.m, Akhem sat down in a chair in the cell, staring at Bennabi, who lolled, gasping, on the waterboard.

"That's enough."

Akhem dried off and looked the subject over. He then walked into the hallway outside the cell and opened his attache case. He extracted a large scalpel and returned, closing the door behind him.

Bennabi's bleary eyes stared at the weapon as Akhem walked forward. The subject leaned away. Akhem nodded and his assistants took the prisoner by the shoulders, one of them grasping his arm

Connections 8   THE GIFT OF TIME   Paul Stuart

hard, rendering it immobile. Akhem took the subject's fingers and leaned forward with the knife.

"Where is the weapon?" he growled. "You have no idea of the pain you'll experience if you don't tell me! Where is it? Who is behind the attack? Tell me!"

Bennabi looked into his eyes. He said nothing. The interrogator moved the blade closer.

It was then that the door burst open.

"Stop!" cried Colonel Peterson. "Come out here into the hallway."

The interrogator paused and stood back. He wiped sweat from his forehead. The three interrogators left the cell and joined the colonel in the hallway.

"I just heard from London. They've found out who Benaabi was meeting in Tunis. They're sending me the information in a few minutes. I want you to hold off until we know more."

Akhem hesitated. Reluctantly he put the scalpel away. Then the large man stared at the CCTV screen, on which was an image of Benaabi sitting in the chair, breathing heavily, staring back into the camera.

The interrogator shook his head. "Not a word. He didn't say a single word."

SATURDAY
■■■

Connections 8   THE GIFT OF TIME   Paul Stuart

At 2 p.m., on the day the weapon would be deployed, Colonel Jim Peterson was alone in his office in the rehabilitation centre, awaiting the secure information about the meeting in Tunis. Armed with that detail, they would have a much better chance to convince Benaabi to give them information.

Come on, he urged, staring at his computer, and a moment later it complied. The computer pinged and he opened the encrypted e-mail from the skinny man he'd met with on Monday. It seemed an ago.

Colonel: we've indentified the people Benaabi met with. But it's not a terrorist cell; it's a human rights group called Humanity Now. We double-checked and our local contacts are sure they're the ones who're behind the weapon. We've followed the group for years and have no indication that it's a cover for a terrorist organization. Discontinue all interrogation until we know more.

Peterson frowned. He knew Humanity Now. Everybody believed it to be a legitimate organization. My God, was all this a misunderstanding? Had Benaabi met with a group about a matter that was completely innocent?

What've we done?

Connections 8   THE GIFT OF TIME   Paul Stuart

He was about to call his superiors and ask for more details when he happened to glance at the computer and saw that he'd received another e-mail. This was from a well-known newspaper. The header "Reporter requesting comment before publication."

He opened the message.

Colonel Peterson. I'm a reporter with the New York Daily Herald. I'm filing the attached article in a few hours with my newspaper. It will run there and in syndication in about two hundred other papers around the world. I'm giving you the opportunity to include a comment, if you wish. I've also sent copies to the White House, the CIA and the Pentagon, seeking their comments, too.

Oh my God. What the hell is that?

With trembling hands the colonel opened the attachment and, to his utter horror, read:

'ROME, MAY 22: A private American company, with ties to the US Government, has been running an illegal operation south of the city, for the purpose of kidnapping, interrogating and occasionally torturing citizens of other countries to extract information from them.

The facility, known in military circles as a black site, is owned by a Reston, Virginia,

Connections 8   THE GIFT OF TIME   Paul Stuart

corporation, Intelligence Analysis Services Inc., whose corporate documents list government security consulting as its main purpose.

Italian business filings state that the purpose of the Roman facility is physical rehabilitation, but no requisite government permits for health care operations have been obtained with respect to it. Further, no licensed rehabilitation professionals are employed by the company, which is owned by a Caribbean subsidiary of IAS. Employees are US and other non-Italian nationals with backgrounds not in medical science but in military and security services.

The operation was conducted without any knowledge on the part of the Italian government and the Italian ambassador to the United States has stated he will demand a full explanation as to why the illegal operation was conducted on Italian soil. Officials from the Polizia di Stato and the Minstero delia Giustizia likewise have promised a full investigation.

There is no direct connection between the US government and the facility outside of Rome. But over the course of the past week, this reporter conducted extensive surveillance of the rehabilitation facility, and observed the presence of a man identified as former Colonel James Peterson, the President of IAS. He is regularly seen in the

Connections 8   THE GIFT OF TIME   Paul Stuart

company of high – ranking Pentagon, CIA and White House officials in the Washington DC area.'

Peterson's satellite phone began ringing.
He supposed the slim man from Washington was calling. Or maybe his boss. Or maybe the White House. Caller ID does not work on encrypted phones. His jaw quivering, he ignored the phone and pressed ahead with the article.

'The discovery of the IAS facility in Rome came about on a tip last week from Humanity Now, a human rights group based in North Africa and long opposed to the use of torture and black sites. The group reported that an Algerian journalist was to be kidnapped in Algiers and transported to a black site somewhere in Europe.
At the same time the human rights organization gave this reporter the name of a number of individuals suspected of being black site interrogators. By examining public records and various travel documents, it was determined that several of these specialists, two US military officers and a mercenary soldier based in Africa, travelled to Rome not long after the journalist's abduction in Algiers.
▪▪

Connections 8   THE GIFT OF TIME   Paul Stuart

Reporters were able to follow the interrogators to the rehabilitation facility, which was then determined to be owned by IAS.'

Slumping in his chair, Peterson ignored the phone. He gave a grim laugh, closing his eyes.

The whole thing, the whole story about terrorists, about the weapon, about Benaabi was a set-up. Yes, there was an 'enemy', but it was merely the human rights group, which had conspired with the professor to expose the black site operation to the press, and the world.

Peterson understood perfectly. Humanity Now had probably been tracking the main interrogators IAS used (Andrew, Claire, Akhem and others) for months, if not years. The group and Benaabi, a human rights activist, had planted the story about the weapon themselves to engineer his kidnapping, then alerted that reporter for the New York newspaper, who leapt after the story of a lifetime.

Benaabi was merely bait, and I went right for it. Of course, he remained silent all the time. That was his job. To draw as many interrogators here as he could and give the reporter a chance to follow them, discover the facility and find out who was behind it.
▪▪▪

Connections 8   THE GIFT OF TIME   Paul Stuart

Oh, this was bad. This was terrible. It was the kind of scandal that could bring down governments. It would certainly end his career. And many others.

It might very likely end the process of black sites altogether, or at least set them back years. He thought about calling the staff together and telling them to destroy all the incriminating papers and flee. But why bother? He reflected. It was too late now.

Peterson decided there was nothing to do but accept his fate. Though he did call the guards and tell them to arrange to have Jacques Benaabi transferred back home. The enemy had won. And, in an odd way, Peterson respected that.

"And make sure he arrives unharmed."

"Yes, sir."

Peterson sat back, hearing in his thoughts the words of the man from Washington.

The weapon…it can do quote 'significant damage.'

Except that there was no weapon. It was all a fake. Yet, with another sour laugh, Peterson decided this wasn't exactly true.

There was a goddam weapon. It wasn't nuclear or chemical or explosive, but in the end was far more effective than any of those and would indeed do significant damage.

Connections 8   THE GIFT OF TIME   Paul Stuart

Thinking about his prisoner's refusal to speak during his captivity, thinking, too, on the devastating paragraphs of the reporter's article, the colonel reflected: the weapon was silence. The weapon was words.

The weapon was truth, and it had taken a long time to realise it.

■■■